COG & COMPASS

GEARED TOWARDS
LONER

ZOTIQUEST GAMES

INTRODUCTION 3
THE COG & COMPASS ERA (1880'S) 5
CHARACTERS 10
RULES..21
CLOCKWORK AUGMENTATIONS 27
COGWORK FAMILIARS.. 28
AIRSHIPS 35
STEAMBOATS..41
LAND VEHICLES 47
EXPLORING THE WORLD 51
URBAN ADVENTURES... 53
SETTING INFORMATION 55
FACTIONS & ORGANIZATIONS.. 60
THE GREAT POWERS OF THE COG & COMPASS ERA............... 63
ADVENTURE TABLES 70
CREATURES & FOES (D66) 94
APPENDIX: INSPIRATIONAL MEDIA................................... 103

A big thank you to the Loner Facebook group and the Orizzonti GDR community for their moral support and patience during the development of this game

Cog & Compass

(CC) 2024 Roberto Bisceglie

Cog & Compass is a solo tabletop RPG adventure set in a world powered by steam and clockwork. Take on the role of a daring inventor tinkering with wondrous automata, a fearless airship captain navigating treacherous skies, or a cunning rogue navigating the bustling underbelly of smog-choked cities.

This minimalist system uses only dice and your imagination. Ask closed-ended questions to an "Oracle" (a system of interpreting dice rolls) to shape your story and uncover intriguing mysteries within the Cog & Compass Era. Be prepared for unexpected twists – the ever-turning gears of fate may surprise you at every turn!

INTRODUCTION

Cog & Compass follows the following design principles:

- Portable: to play you will need a few common (six-sided) dice and writing materials. Anything else is optional and not essential.
- Rules-Light: the game relies on a few rules and only one solving mechanic, easy to learn and eventually to memorize.
- Tag-based: characters and situations are defined only by qualitative descriptors and no quantitative characteristics.

With a focus on quick resolutions, Cog & Compass throws you headfirst into the heart of the action. Your character will be defined by thematic tags, allowing you to craft a hero that perfectly embodies the spirit of the age - be it a "Brilliant Engineer" or a "Cunning Spymaster."

WHAT IS A ROLE PLAYING GAME (RPG)?

A role-playing game (RPG) is a type of game in which players assume the roles of fictional characters and act out their actions and decisions within a narrative or imaginary setting. The outcome of these actions and decisions is often determined by a set of rules and game mechanics, such as dice rolls or statistical attributes of the characters. Players may also collaborate to create a shared story or narrative through their characters' actions and interactions.

WHAT IS A SOLO RPG?

In a solo RPG a single player takes on the roles of one or more characters, while also simultaneously managing some elements of the game world. These games typically involve the use of a rule system and game mechanics to determine the outcome of actions taken by the player-controlled characters. Unlike a gamebook (such as the Fighting Fantasy, Lone Wolf, and Tunnels & Trolls series) a solo RPG is not a form of interactive, forked narrative in which outcomes are predetermined and limited by the author's choices.

Through the interaction of player, oracle, tools, and prompts, the character's actions will build an emergent narrative within whose boundaries anything can be attempted, without predetermined limits.

SAFETY TOOLS

You will play alone, but be sure to play in an environment that is comfortable for you, without overexerting yourself, and reserve the option to stop as soon as you feel uncomfortable for any reason, physical or emotional. Don't be afraid to tackle new themes, but do so in full awareness of your boundaries.

MINIMUM REQUIREMENTS

To play *Cog & Compass* you will need:

- **4 six sided dice (also known as d6s):** two pairs of different colors
- **Paper and writing tools:** at least a sheet of scrap paper and and pencil, but index cards or sticky notes are a fine addition
- **Character sheet:** you may use the provided sheet at the back or a simple index card.
- **Notebook:** Cog & Compass is not a solo journaling game, you can easily play it in the "theater of mind". But you can keep track of you game if you feel the need!

THE COG & COMPASS ERA (1880's)

The Point of Divergence: The Great Exhibition in London (1851) showcases not just marvels of industry, but a revolution: the Analytical Engine, a steam-powered calculating machine capable of complex mathematical equations. This invention ignites a new age of innovation. Gifted engineers like Charles Babbage and Ada Lovelace become national heroes, ushering in the Cog & Compass Era.

Steam Power Reigns Supreme: Coal fuels the world. Gigantic steam engines power factories, automata servants tend to the wealthy, and towering smokestacks pierce the skies of bustling metropolises. Technological advancements based on clock-work and steam create marvels like:

The World: Welcome to the Cog & Compass Era, a world where the 1850s ushered in a technological revolution fueled by steam. Nations of the real 19th century have embraced this power, reshaping industry, culture, and igniting a race for dominance in the skies.

STEAM-POWERED PROGRESS

- **Analytical Engines:** These monstrous machines crunch data, solve complex equations, and assist in engineering marvels.
- **Automata:** Clockwork servants are commonplace, performing everything from menial tasks to intricate surgery. Advanced models converse and respond to sophisticated commands.
- **Airships:** The sky teems with colossal steam-powered vessels, transporting goods, people, and military might. Each nation boasts a unique fleet design, a testament to their technological prowess and national identity.
- **Communication Revolution:** Steam-powered pneumatic tubes and telegraph lines weave a web of rapid communication across the globe.

THE GREAT POWERS

1. **The British Empire:** A titan of steam technology, Britain leads the world in automata and calculation engines. London, a sprawling metropolis choked with smog, showcases feats of brass and iron engineering.
2. **The German Confederation:** Rivaling Britain, Germany boasts robust engineering institutions and powerful steam-powered machinery that dominate their industry and war machine.

3. **The United States of America:** Fueled by steam innovation, America witnesses rapid expansion, especially in agriculture and manufacturing. New York and Chicago are bustling hubs of steam technology, with airships a common sight on their crowded skylines.
4. **The French Republic:** France prioritizes aesthetics and cultural advancement with steam. Paris, a city of art nouveau and industrial chic, boasts steam-powered art galleries, theaters, and bustling cafes.
5. **The Japanese Empire:** A recent addition to the global stage, Japan seamlessly blends steam technology with their traditions. Unique steam-powered samurai armor and weaponry bolster their military and cultural identity.
6. **The Tsarist Empire:** Russia seeks to catch up with its rivals by pouring resources into research and development, focusing on brute force and size in its automata and airship designs.

A WORLD IN FLUX

- **Class Division:** Rapid technological growth has created a stark class division based on access to steam technology. The wealthy flaunt their personalized automata and exclusive airship clubs, while the working class toils in factories fueled by coal and sweat.
- **Social Change:** Thinkers, writers, and artists grapple with the social and ethical implications of this new mechanical and societal power.
- **Workers' Rights:** As automata replace human labor, the working class struggles for rights and fair treatment.

ADVENTURE AWAITS

The Cog & Compass Era offers boundless opportunities for adventure:

- **Espionage & Intrigue:** Unravel conspiracies and outmaneuver rival agents in the shadows of global powers.
- **Exploration & Discovery:** Embark on expeditions into uncharted territories with advanced steam-powered maps and the latest airships.
- **Social Upheaval:** Champion the rights of the working class or navigate the ethical quandaries surrounding automata.
- **Invention Contests:** Showcase your engineering brilliance in prestigious competitions where the next groundbreaking steam-powered innovation awaits.

In this world of gears, pistons, and soaring ambitions, what will your role be?

PLAYABLE THEMES

Exploration & Discovery:

- Lead expeditions into uncharted territories with steam-powered airships.
- Unravel ancient mysteries using clockwork devices and advanced analytical engines.
- Chart new trade routes and discover valuable resources for the burgeoning steam economy.

Espionage & Intrigue:

- Navigate the treacherous world of international diplomacy in the Global Steam Council.
- Unmask plots and conspiracies involving stolen steam technology or sabotage.
- Infiltrate heavily guarded facilities to acquire vital information or secure powerful artifacts.

Social Change & Revolution:

- Champion the rights of the working class struggling against automata replacing their jobs.
- Advocate for the ethical treatment of automata and fight for their recognition as sentient beings.
- Spark a social movement challenging the status quo and the power of the industrial elite.

Technological Innovation:

- Design and build groundbreaking steam-powered inventions that could change the world.
- Participate in prestigious invention contests and showcase your engineering brilliance.
- Push the boundaries of steam technology, exploring uncharted territories of science and mechanics.

Mystery & Crime:

- Investigate a series of seemingly unrelated incidents and uncover a hidden conspiracy.
- Track down a notorious airship pirate who preys on unsuspecting merchant vessels.
- Solve a baffling murder where the prime suspect is a sophisticated clockwork automaton.

Moral Dilemmas & Choices:

- Grapple with the ethical implications of using bio-mechanical creatures for war or entertainment.
- Decide whether to help or exploit an automata struggling with its identity and yearning for freedom.
- Choose between loyalty to your nation and the greater good as international tensions rise.

TIMELINE

- **1851:** The Great Exhibition in London unveils the Analytical Engine, a revolutionary steam-powered calculating machine. This ignites the Cog & Compass Era.
- **1853-1856:**
  - The Great Powers race to develop their own Analytical Engines and automata technology.
  - The first commercially available automata for domestic use appear, causing a stir among the wealthy.
  - 1857: The American inventor Elijah Otis unveils the steam-powered elevator, revolutionizing architecture and urban development.
- **1860-1865:** The American Civil War is fought with a mix of traditional and innovative steam-powered weaponry, including armored trains and early prototype airships. The Union's superior use of steam technology proves decisive.
- **1863:** French engineer Jules Verne publishes "Five Weeks in a Balloon," sparking a global fascination with aerial exploration.
- **1869:** The completion of the Transcontinental Railroad in the US is achieved significantly faster due to steam-powered construction equipment.
- **1870-1871:** The Franco-Prussian War sees the first large-scale deployment of steam-powered tanks and armored airships. Prussia's superior technology secures victory.
- **1873:** The Great Airship Race is held in London, showcasing the latest innovations in airship design and navigation. The American entry, the "Eagle's Flight," takes first place.
- **1875-1880:** A gold rush erupts in the previously unexplored Congo Basin, fueled by the need for resources to power the growing steam infrastructure. Tensions rise between the Great Powers vying for control.
- **1877:** The Indian Rebellion utilizes stolen and re-purposed British automata, leading to a brutal conflict. The event sparks debate about the ethics of automata warfare.
- **1882:** The world's first international communication network is established using a combination of steam-powered pneumatic tubes and telegraph lines.
- **1885:** Labor unrest grows in major industrial cities as automata replace human workers. Strikes and protests erupt across Europe and America.

- **1886-1887:** The "Age of Exploration" reaches new heights as steam-powered airships allow expeditions into previously unreachable regions of the Arctic, Amazon, and Africa. Uncharted territories are mapped, and valuable resources are discovered.
- **1887 (Present):** The Cog & Compass Era is in full swing. The world is a tapestry of steam, steel, and innovation. Airships dominate the skies, automata serve in homes and factories, and the Great Powers compete for technological supremacy. Social tensions simmer as the working class struggles for rights and a place in this rapidly changing world.

THE COG & COMPASS ERA   **9**

CHARACTERS

Before you venture up into the skies, over the seas, or across the lands of the Cog & Compass era, let's see how to manage your Protagonist and other characters.

EVERYTHING IS A CHARACTER!

In *Cog & Compass* Non-Playing Characters (NPCs), Foes, Organizations, Monsters, and even relevant objects like vehicles are characters too!

Your Protagonist is described by some fixed traits:

- **Name:** The name should be iconic and consistent with the tone and setting of the story.
- **Concept:** A concise description of the character's profession, background, and abilities. The best are adjective-name pairings, like "Venturous Smuggler" or "Child Prodigy".
- Skills (x2): Abilities not necessarily character-specific but not characteristics common to all. "Smart" is not a skill, "Engine Whisperer" is.
- **Frailty:** Something that could potentially get in the way of the character, either physically, mentally, or socially.
- Gear (x2): Particular equipment supplied to the character in coherence with the setting. Everyday items are taken for granted and do not fall under this trait.
- **Goal:** The long-term objective.
- **Motive:** What drives the pursuit of the goal.
- **Nemesis:** A person or organization that hinders the protagonist. It can emerge during the first game sessions, it may or may or not be the direct antagonist of the story, ready to appear to make life even more difficult
- Luck: The measure of a character's ability to avoid ill fortune or an inauspicious outcome. It applies only in Conflicts and automatically recharges when they end. Luck starts and caps at 6.

These traits are described by tags, descriptive words or phrases that can identify anything in the game world. Even the details of the environment in which the action moves and conditions (physical or mental) of the characters are tags.

They are qualitative representations. They are not quantitative measures.

You can use the following traits to create a character on the fly, mix them, or just use them as inspiration.

CONCEPTS

	⚀	⚁	⚂
⚀	Airship Captain	Ingenious Inventor	Street Urchin
⚁	Sky Pirate	Master Tinkerer	Detective
⚂	Mechanical Savant	Mechanical Engineer	Investigative Journalist
⚃	Aeronautic Explorer	Clockwork Artisan	Private Investigator
⚄	Gadgetsmith	Steam Mechanic	Cipher Expert
⚅	Sky Smuggler	Renowned Inventor	Steampunk Detective
	⚃	⚄	⚅
⚀	Eccentric Scholar	Mysterious Agent	Clockwork Spy
⚁	Socialite	Secret Society Operative	Automaton Prototype
⚂	Factory Worker	Underground Revolutionary	Steam-Powered Alchemist
⚃	Inventor's Assistant	Saboteur	Steam Dynamics Expert
⚄	Aristocrat	Underground Informant	Airship Engineer
⚅	Noble Outcast	Saboteur's Accomplice	Industrial Innovator

SKILLS

⚀	⚁	⚂
⚀ Piloting	Engineering	Stealth
⚁ Gunmanship	Invention	Investigation
⚂ Survival	Mechanical Repair	Deduction
⚃ Navigation	Clockwork Crafting	Observation
⚄ Acrobatics	Technological Lore	Research
⚅ Aerial Maneuvers	Automaton Design	Forensics

⚃	⚄	⚅
⚀ Diplomacy	Espionage	Mechanical Repair
⚁ Etiquette	Sabotage	Steam Control
⚂ Persuasion	Codebreaking	Steam Manipulation
⚃ Seduction	Infiltration	Steam Resonance
⚄ Networking	Disguise	Steam Channeling
⚅ Public Speaking	Deception	Steam Augmentation

FRAILTIES

	⚀	⚁	⚂
⚀	Fear of Heights	Clockwork Obsession	Technological Hallucinations
⚁	Fear of Disassembly	Mechanical Malfunction	Chronic Respiratory Illness
⚂	Impaired Decision-Making	Risky Gambler	Gullibility
⚃	Impulsive Behavior	Abandonment Issues	Speech Impediment
⚄	Tendency to Faint	Inability to Keep Secrets	Insomnia
⚅	PTSD from Automaton Encounter	Prone to Panic Attacks	Fear of Rejection

	⚃	⚄	⚅
⚀	Memory Loss	Easily Distracted	Fear of Clocks
⚁	Mechanophobia	Aversion to Modern Clothing	Chronic Nostalgia
⚂	Industrial Allergy	Uncontrolled Tinkering	Mismatched Limbs
⚃	Self-Doubt	Aversion to Fire	Impaired Smell
⚄	Paranoia	Crippling Guilt	Impaired Hearing
⚅	Perpetual Cynicism	Obsessive Need for Order	Germaphobia

GEAR

	⚀	⚁	⚂
⚀	Tesla Rifle	Steam-Powered Arm	Toolbelt
⚁	Airship Model	Gadgetry Kit	Mechanical Pet
⚂	Zeppelin Map	Jetpack	Spyglass
⚃	Smoke Bombs	Pocket Watch	Technological Codex
⚄	Aether Compass	Gear Gauntlet	Notebook
⚅	Clockwork Automaton	Stealth Cloak	Mechanical Limb

	⚃	⚄	⚅
⚀	Monocle	Revolver	Grappling Hook
⚁	Wrist-mounted Dart	Cipher Ring	Steam Focus
⚂	Codebook	Automaton Companion	Steam Conduit
⚃	Walking Stick	Gas Mask	Steam Battery
⚄	Fine Attire	Disguise Kit	Steam Amplifier
⚅	Detonator	Concealed Holster	Steam Capacitor

MALE

	⚀	⚁	⚂
⚀	Nathaniel	Ezekiel	Thaddeus
⚁	Ignatius	Percival	Bartholomew
⚂	Horatio	Phineas	Cornelius
⚃	Alaric	Barnaby	Casimir
⚄	Cornelius	Thaddeus	Linus
⚅	Ambrose	Ignatius	Remington

	⚃	⚄	⚅
⚀	Archibald	Theodore	Benedict
⚁	Leopold	Reginald	Octavius
⚂	Montgomery	Atticus	Maximilian
⚃	Reginald	Sylvester	Percival
⚄	Phineas	Archibald	Bartholomew
⚅	Alaric	Percival	Augustus

FEMALE

	⚀	⚁	⚂
⚀	Amelia	Clara	Isabella
⚁	Ada	Eliza	Matilda
⚂	Sophia	Josephine	Arabella
⚃	Octavia	Millicent	Rosalind
⚄	Evangeline	Ophelia	Felicity
⚅	Theodora	Harriet	Philomena
	⚃	⚄	⚅
⚀	Penelope	Victoria	Evelyn
⚁	Beatrice	Lillian	Genevieve
⚂	Prudence	Winifred	Imogen
⚃	Adeline	Cecilia	Seraphina
⚄	Gwendolyn	Rosamund	Vivienne
⚅	Clementine	Georgiana	Cordelia

SURNAMES

	⚀ (1)	⚁ (2)	⚂ (3)
⚀ (1)	Thorne	Ironsmith	Pendleton
⚁ (2)	Steamson	Whitlock	Wraithborne
⚂ (3)	Ironclad	Windermere	Clockwright
⚃ (4)	Cogswell	Thornfield	Brassington
⚄ (5)	Steamwell	Clockburn	Ironhaven
⚅ (6)	Blacksmith	Gearhart	Pendulum

	⚃ (4)	⚄ (5)	⚅ (6)
⚀ (1)	Gearhart	Cogsworth	Brasswick
⚁ (2)	Blackthorn	Copperfield	Gearwright
⚂ (3)	Stoker	Redforge	Gearspring
⚃ (4)	Steelgrave	Hightower	Gearsmith
⚄ (5)	Steamwhisper	Gearstone	Brassfield
⚅ (6)	Ironwright	Copperhill	Windforge

NICKNAMES

	⚀	⚁	⚂
⚀	Cogmaster	Bolt	Steamwright
⚁	Smokestack	Rivet	Flywheel
⚂	Brasshand	The Tinkerer	Volt
⚃	Clockwork	Sprocket	Copperpot
⚄	Steamsmith	Oilcan	Gasket
⚅	The Mechanist	Aether	Pressure

	⚃	⚄	⚅
⚀	Irons	Gearhead	Piston
⚁	Spark	Boiler	Coalfoot
⚂	Widget	Fuse	Steambeard
⚃	Crankshaft	Valve	Locomotive
⚄	Springheel	Ironclad	Treadturner
⚅	Blacksmoke	Dynamo	Piston Pete

RULES

Cog & Compass is a minimalist Solo Role Playing Game designed to be played with only one character (the Protagonist). You'll guide them through the story that will unravel during the game, asking closed questions to an Oracle which will help you overturn your expectations.

Every now and then you will be surprised with an unexpected twist!

KEEP THE ACTION IN MOTION

A game in *Cog & Compass* is a succession of scenes. A scene is a unit of time in which a certain action takes place in pursuit of a certain short-term goal.

In *Cog & Compass* at each scene: 1. Identify what you expect from the scene. Compared to traits, goal, and motivation determine the Protagonist's action. What might be the reaction of the game world? 2. Test your expectations. When you are uncertain (or overconfident) about the reaction to your actions, ask the Oracle a closed question (answer is Yes or No), considering the tags involved to determine if there is an Advantage or Disadvantage. 3. Interpret the result. Is the Oracle's answer in line with your expectations? If not, in the context in which the scene takes place, how should an answer that subverts them be considered?

This sequence will come to you naturally after some practice. Use it as a guideline the first few times.

CONSULTING THE ORACLE

When you need to test your expectations you'll ask the Oracle a closed question.

You'll need 2d6 in one color (Chance Dice), and 2d6 in another (Risk Dice).

Dice Value	Chance Die > Risk Die	Risk Die > Chance Die
Both < ⚅	Yes, but...	No, but...
Both > ⚀	Yes, and...	No, and...
Mismatched	Yes	No
Equal	Yes, but... Add 1 to the Twist Counter	

To resolve a closed question, roll one Chance Die and one Risk Die: - If the Chance Die is highest, the answer is Yes. - If the Risk Die is highest, the answer is No. - If both are low (3 or less), add a but.... - If both are high (4 or more), add an and.... - If both are equal, the answer is Yes, and.... Add a point to the Twist Counter.

ADVANTAGE AND DISADVANTAGE

If circumstances or positive tags grant an advantage, add a Chance Die to the roll. Otherwise, when hindrances or negative tag cause a disadvantage, add a Risk Die. In both cases keep only the higher die of the added type when you check the roll.

Consider tags intuitively and not quantitatively, using the context of the situation at play. It is important to keep the flow of play fast and not accounting for advantages and disadvantages numerically!

TWIST COUNTER

The Twist Counter is a measure of the rising tension in the narrative. At the beginning is set to 0. Every time a double throw (dice are equal) happens, add 1 to the Counter. If the Counter is below three, consider the answer as "Yes, but...". Otherwise a Twist happens and resets the Counter.

Roll 2d6 and consult the following Twist Table to determine what kind of twist happens.

D6	Subject	Action
⚀	A third party	Appears
⚁	The hero	Alters the location
⚂	An encounter	Helps the hero
⚃	A physical event	Hinders the hero
⚄	An emotional event	Changes the goal
⚅	An object	Ends the scene

Interpret the two-word sentence in the context of the current scene. Twists will keep the plot and events going in unexpected ways.

STEAM RESONANCE

In this world, characters have a refined sensitivity to the mechanics and flow of steam technology. They possess a "Steam Resonance" (SR) score that quantifies their proficiency and connection with steam-powered devices. This affinity allows characters to perform enhanced actions with technology, but careful management is necessary to avoid the dangers of overheating.

- **Starting Score:** Each character begins with a Steam Resonance score of 6, reflecting their innate ability to interface with steam technology.

- **Using Steam Resonance:** SR can be utilized to amplify physical actions, operate complex steam-driven machinery, or execute unique technological skills specific to each character.

- **Enhanced Actions:** To enhance an action using SR, a player expends one SR point and rolls a die. If the result exceeds their current SR score, the character's device overheats, resulting in negative consequences and failure of the action. If the result is lower or equal, the action succeeds with added benefits (advantage).

- **Recovery of SR Points:** SR points are gradually regained through rest or by spending time in steam-rich environments. Characters naturally recover one SR point per day. Additional recovery methods might involve specific gear or settings designed to quickly rejuvenate steam affinity.

SMOG EXPOSURE

The pervasive smog that blankets industrial areas in this world poses significant risks. This dense air pollution, a byproduct of the widespread reliance on steam and coal, can severely impact health and hinder navigation.

- **Effects of Smog:** Characters exposed to smog without appropriate protection may experience several detrimental effects:
  - **Reduced Visibility:** Thick smog decreases visibility, complicating combat and exploration activities.
  - **Respiratory Issues:** Prolonged exposure can diminish stamina and overall health due to the inhalation of toxic particulates.
  - **Cognitive Impairments:** Some may suffer from disorientation or hallucinations, affecting decision-making or causing them to see illusions.
- **Protective Measures:**
  - **Gear:** Utilizing items like gas masks or air filtration devices can lessen or neutralize the effects of smog.
  - **Antidotes and Treatments:** Certain concoctions or medical treatments can alleviate the symptoms caused by smog exposure.
  - **Advanced Equipment:** Crafting or acquiring high-quality protective gear provides stronger resistance or even immunity to specific penalties associated with smog.
- **Navigational and Quest Challenges:**
  - **Traverse Smoggy Areas:** Characters must either prepare thoroughly (e.g., ensuring sufficient protective gear and antidotes) or find alternative pathways to avoid the worst of the smog.
  - **Unique Quest Opportunities:** Smoggy zones can be the setting for diverse missions—investigating the source of the smog, initiating cleanup operations, or rescuing inhabitants and workers suffering from severe smog exposure.

CONFLICTS

A Conflict is any situation in which opponents clash, attacking, defending, or wearing each other down in order to win. This applies both in a practical and metaphorical sense.

So, a Conflict is not only limited to combat (or fighting) in the strict sense but also to competitive situations (such as contests, duels, verbal confrontations, etc.) in which two or more characters (including vehicles, of course!) compete.

Conflicts can be resolved in different ways depending on preferences and context: 1. Ask a single closed question. The Oracle's answer determines the outcome of the conflict. 2. Ask a series of closed questions to resolve current single actions. 3. Use the rules of Harm & Luck below.

Note that the Twist Counter does not apply to Harm & Luck. Instead, it is used regularly if the Conflict is handled with closed questions.

If the conflict is resolved by applying damage to the Luck trait, roll the dice to determine whether the protagonist causes damage to the opponent or suffers damage due to counterattack or failed defense. The rolls are player facing only.

The damage reduces the Luck of the target, whether protagonist or NPC. When the Luck runs out, the character has lost the conflict.

The final outcome depends on the context. Do you get caught? Are you seriously injured? You may even die if that fits the narrative.

Answer	Do you get what you want?	Harm
Yes, and...	You get what you want, and something else.	Cause 3
Yes...	You get what you want.	Cause 2
Yes, but...	You get what you want, but at a cost.	Cause 1
No, but...	You don't get what you want, but it's not a total loss.	Take 1
No...	You don't get what you were after.	Take 2
No, and...	You don't get what you want, and things get worse.	Take 3

DETERMINE THE MOOD OF THE NEXT SCENE

At the end of the current scene sometimes you will be clear about the direction to take, other times you may need to determine the general mood of the next one. In this case roll 1d6 and consult the following table:

D6	Next Scene
1 - 3	Dramatic scene
4 - 5	Quiet Scene
6	Meanwhile...

- A dramatic scene does not break the tension of the previous scene but carries it further forward, introducing further obstacles or difficulties.
- During a quiet scene there is time to take a breath, to heal, to make plans for the next steps and to deepen relationships.
- A meanwhile scene takes place somewhere else, other than where the hero is. It cuts to villains or other plot-important characters.

OPEN-ENDED QUESTION OR GET INSPIRED

To answer an Open-Ended question, roll 1d6 once on each of the following tables (roll at least a verb and a noun, adjectives are optional).

WHEN THE STORY ENDS

At the end of the adventure you may add another trait to the character. It is better that this is related to how the story just ended and can be either a Skill, Gear, a new Frailty, or even a new Nemesis! You can also modify an existing trait to better represent an enhanced expertise.

Also update the list of NPCs, Locations, and Events that may show up again in future adventures.

CLOCKWORK AUGMENTATIONS

Characters can enhance their abilities through clockwork augmentations. These range from steam-powered limbs that increase strength to cog-driven optics that sharpen perception. However, over-dependence on augmentations might result in the loss of organic abilities.

1. **Cogspring Legs:** Increases a character's speed and jump height, enabling breathtaking leaps or rapid sprints over short distances.

2. **Steamfist Gauntlets:** Enhances strength, allowing for devastating punches capable of bending metal or shattering stone.

3. **Opti-Gear Eyes:** Grants superior vision, including the ability to zoom or see in low light conditions, making the wearer an exceptional scout or sniper.

4. **Gearwork Wings:** A pair of mechanical wings that enable short-duration flight or extended gliding, perfect for reaching elevated places or making dramatic entrances.

5. **Pneumatic Arms:** Provide immense lifting capacity and crushing power, ideal for heavy labor or breaking through barriers.

6. **Vocal Modulator:** Allows the user to mimic any voice heard previously or amplify their own, useful for deception or commanding attention.

7. **Chrono-Link Bracelet:** Enhances reaction time to near-instantaneous levels for a few seconds, simulating a brief period of perceived time dilation.

8. **Echo-Locator Ears:** Sonar-based augmentation granting echolocation, enabling navigation and detection of objects or beings through solid walls or in complete darkness.

9. **Smoke Filtration Lungs:** Offer protection against smog, gas attacks, and respiratory toxins, filtering out harmful particles and converting them into breathable air.

10. **Auto-Repairing Skin:** A mesh of fine clockwork and nanogears beneath the skin that gradually repairs wounds, reducing healing time.

11. **Wind-Up Heart:** A backup heart that kicks in if the original fails, providing a second chance at life in dire circumstances.

12. **Gyro-Balanced Core:** Improves balance and agility, allowing the user to perform acrobatic feats or maintain their footing in combat on uneven terrain.

13. **Steam-Boosted Sensors:** Heighten all five senses, offering superhuman perception that can detect subtle changes in a person's heartbeat or track quarry by scent alone.
14. **Circuit-Weave Brain:** Enhances cognitive functions with clockwork precision, boosting problem-solving abilities, calculation speed, and overall mental acuity.
15. **Hydraulic Crunch Claws:** Replace the hands with powerful clamps capable of crushing or manipulating heavy objects, while retaining fine motor control for delicate tasks.
16. **Mnemonic Storage Drive:** Implanted in the brain, this device significantly increases memory capacity and recall speed, making the user a walking library of information.
17. **Pressure-Powered Jump Boots:** These rugged, steam-driven boots utilize high-pressure steam bursts to allow for explosive leaps, enabling characters to navigate treacherous terrains or overcome obstacles with ease. Perfect for quick escapes or reaching difficult places.
18. **Cognitive Gear Processor:** This sophisticated clockwork mechanism is integrated into the cerebral cortex, enhancing decision-making speeds and providing a tactical edge by calculating multiple probabilities and outcomes in real-time, akin to a human chess computer.

COGWORK FAMILIARS

Characters can have cogwork animal companions. These steam-powered familiars can assist in various tasks, from scouting to combat. Players need to manage their familiars' steam reserves and perform maintenance.

- Players can design their cogwork familiars, choosing from various animal forms that offer different abilities. For example, a cogwork owl could provide enhanced vision for scouting, while a cogwork wolf might offer combat support.
- Familiars require steam to operate. Their steam reserves deplete with use and must be replenished through specific resources or by resting in a steam-enriched environment.
- Regular maintenance is required to keep familiars operational. Neglect could lead to malfunctions or decreased efficiency in tasks.
- Players can upgrade their familiars with parts obtained from quests, crafting, or trade, enhancing their abilities or adding new functions.

COGWORK FAMILIAR TRAITS

	⚀	⚁	⚂
⚀	Clockwork Cat	Sentinel Owl	Scout Mouse
⚁	Steam Serpent	Mechanical Hawk	Recon Rabbit
⚂	Gearwork Horse	Loadbearing Beetle	Surveyor Squirrel
⚃	Locomotive Lynx	Aqua Explorer Fish	Treasure Tracker Magpie
⚄	Miner Mole	Pathfinder Pigeon	Navigator Nightingale
⚅	Explorer Elephant	Heavy-Duty Tortoise	Climber Chameleon

	⚃	⚄	⚅
⚀	Guard Dog	Messenger Raven	Surveillance Spider
⚁	Battle Badger	Signal Fox	Illuminator Firefly
⚂	Protector Panther	Helper Monkey	Guide Parrot
⚃	Combat Crab	Informant Bat	Constructor Beaver
⚄	Sentinel Swan	Courier Cheetah	Reconnaissance Rooster
⚅	Spy Seal	Alert Albatross	Maintenance Meerkat

SKILLS

⚀	⚁	⚂
⚀ Enhanced Vision	Night Vision	Enhanced Hearing
⚁ Silent Movement	High Altitude Flight	Rapid Burrowing
⚂ Load Carrying	Terrain Adaptation	High Speed Scouting
⚃ Fast Recovery	Water Navigation	Item Retrieval
⚄ Deep Earth Navigation	Urban Navigation	Air Navigation
⚅ Heavy Lifting	Environmental Resistance	Camouflage

⚃	⚄	⚅
⚀ Enhanced Smell	Speed Boost	Heightened Reflexes
⚁ Strong Defense	Long Range Signal	Illumination
⚂ Protective Alert	Intricate Manipulation	Vocal Mimicry
⚃ Crowd Control	Stealth Operation	Construction Assistance
⚄ Water Surveillance	Emergency Messaging	Detailed Mapping
⚅ Cold Endurance	Storm Endurance	Self-Repairing

FRAILTIES

	⚀	⚁	⚂
⚀	Overheating	Noise Sensitivity	Light Sensitivity
⚁	High Energy Consumption	Limited Range	Frequent Maintenance
⚂	Rusting	Cold Intolerance	Dust Susceptibility
⚃	Component Wear	Battery Dependency	Signal Disruption
⚄	Maintenance Intensive	Hack Vulnerability	Collision Vulnerability
⚅	Fuel Dependency	Specific Habitat Needs	Power Surge Vulnerability

	⚃	⚄	⚅
⚀	Moisture Damage	Limited Operation Time	Fragile Mechanics
⚁	Low Power Mode	Magnetic Interference	Signal Jamming
⚂	High Light Glare	Fragile Exterior	Limited Mobility
⚃	Overload Risk	System Reboot Delay	Navigation Errors
⚄	Sensory Overload	Memory Corruption	Instruction Misinterpretation
⚅	Balance Issues	Structural Weakness	Environmental Sensitivity

GEAR

	⚀	⚁	⚂
⚀	Optical Enhancers	Stealth Coating	Audio Boosters
⚁	Communication Devices	Flight Enhancements	Burrowing Gear
⚂	Carrying Harness	All-Terrain Treads	Mapping Sensors
⚃	Repair Kits	Waterproof Covers	Retrieval Magnets
⚄	Navigation Systems	Urban Gear	Aerial Maneuver Gear
⚅	Heavy-Duty Cables	Environmental Suits	Adaptive Camouflage

	⚃	⚄	⚅
⚀	Smell Enhancers	Mobility Enhancers	Reflex Enhancers
⚁	Defense Mechanisms	Signal Amplifiers	Light Projectors
⚂	Shock Absorbers	Tool Attachments	Voice Synthesizers
⚃	Crowd Repellents	Camouflage Skins	Building Tools
⚄	Water Propulsion Kits	Emergency Beacons	Topographical Mappers
⚅	Ice Chains	Storm Shields	Self-Diagnostics Kits

EXAMPLES

SCOUTWING SPARROW
- **Concept:** Swift Scout
- **Skills:** Skyline Navigator, Silent Glide
- **Frailty:** Weather-Sensitive
- **Gear:** Optical Lens Monocle, Message Capsule

GUARDHOUND BULLDOG
- **Concept:** Protective Guardian
- **Skills:** Intruder Deterrent, Lockjaw Grip
- **Frailty:** High Maintenance
- **Gear:** Reinforced Plating, Olfactory Enhancer

PUDDLEJUMPER FROG
- **Concept:** Aquatic Explorer
- **Skills:** Amphibious Mobility, Echo Resonance
- **Frailty:** Pollution-Sensitive
- **Gear:** Waterproof Gear Housing, Retrieval Net

WHISKERTWIST MOUSE
- **Concept:** Stealthy Spy
- **Skills:** Wiretap Whiskers, Shadow Scamper
- **Frailty:** Vulnerable Size
- **Gear:** Data Storage Tail, Camouflage Coating

COGTAIL PEACOCK
- **Concept:** Enchanting Performer
- **Skills:** Hypnotic Display, Sonorous Call
- **Frailty:** Elaborate Maintenance
- **Gear:** Visual Effect Feathers, Scent Dispenser

GEARGRINDER OWL
- **Concept:** Nocturnal Watcher
- **Skills:** Night Vision, Silent Surveillance
- **Frailty:** Daylight Ineffective
- **Gear:** Recording Eyes, Signal Jammer Claws

AIRSHIPS

This is a world of airships, where the skies are your domain and adventure awaits at every altitude. The shipyard is where these marvels of engineering and imagination take shape, each vessel designed with a unique purpose and character. From swift explorers to imposing warships, these airships hold the key to your journeys through the boundless heavens.

Certainly! Here's a template filled out with airship traits based on various archetypal roles and features within a steampunk setting. This setup could help define different types of airships that characters might own, command, or encounter.

CONCEPTS

	⚀	⚁	⚂
⚀	Trade Schooner	Arctic Explorer	Royal Vessel
⚁	Cargo Freighter	Storm Chaser	Diplomatic Yacht
⚂	Luxury Liner	Icebreaker	Spymaster's Zeppelin
⚃	Medical Frigate	High-Altitude Surveyor	Cultural Envoy
⚄	Entertainment Palace	Disaster Relief Carrier	Propaganda Blimp
⚅	Mobile Fortress	Wilderness Explorer	Royal Guard Airship

	⚃	⚄	⚅
⚀	Floating Laboratory	Pirate Skiff	Stealth Recon
⚁	Smuggler's Clipper	Gunship Cruiser	Research Vessel
⚂	Prison Transport	Battle Frigate	Weather Monitor
⚃	Treasure Hunter	Patrol Airship	Mining Platform
⚄	Salvage Vessel	Mercenary Carrier	Scientific Expedition
⚅	Transport Behemoth	Rebel Command Ship	High-Atmosphere Probe

COG & COMPASS

SKILLS

	⚀	⚁	⚂
⚀	Enhanced Navigation	Weather Resistance	Diplomatic Suites
⚁	Heavy Cargo Lifting	Storm Navigation	Espionage Equipment
⚂	Luxury Amenities	Ice-Cutting Hull	Secure Communication
⚃	Medical Facilities	High-Altitude Capability	Cultural Exhibits
⚄	Entertainment Systems	Emergency Response Systems	Propaganda Broadcasters
⚅	Siege Weapons	Wilderness Survival Kits	Elite Guard Quarters

	⚃	⚄	⚅
⚀	Advanced Alchemy Labs	Cannon Arrays	Stealth Technology
⚁	Smuggling Compartments	Armored Hull	Long-Range Sensors
⚂	Prisoner Cells	Broadside Cannons	Atmospheric Analysis
⚃	Treasure Scanners	Patrol Radar	Resource Extraction
⚄	Deep Sea Recovery Gear	Mercenary Quarters	Experimental Labs
⚅	Massive Storage	Command Center	High-Atmosphere Communications

FRAILTIES

	⚀	⚁	⚂
⚀	Low Fuel Efficiency	Vulnerable to Ice	High Profile Target
⚁	Slow Speed	Limited Maneuverability in Storms	Known to Diplomats
⚂	Attracts Pirates	Freezes Easily	Easily Bugged
⚃	Frequent Malfunctions	High Fuel Consumption	Cultural Misunderstandings
⚄	Popular Target for Thieves	Slow Emergency Response	Monitored by Authorities
⚅	Siege Weapon Recoil	Struggles in Wilderness	Known Royal Allegiance

	⚃	⚄	⚅
⚀	Sensitive Equipment	Fire Hazard	Radar Signature
⚁	Contraband Risk	High Maintenance	Sensor Interference
⚂	Jailbreak Risk	Loud Engines	Weather Sensitive
⚃	Treasure Hunter Rivalry	Target for Patrols	Rock Debris Damage
⚄	High Salvage Costs	Prone to Mercenary Mutiny	Experimental Malfunctions
⚅	Overloaded Weight Capacity	Rebellious Crew	Communication Blackouts

GEAR

	⚀	⚁	⚂
⚀	Advanced Compass	Reinforced Hull	Diplomatic Codes
⚁	Heavy-Duty Cranes	Storm Shields	Embassy Quarters
⚂	Opulent Decor	Heated Outer Shell	Encrypted Radios
⚃	Hospital Bay	Oxygen Tanks	Cultural Artifacts
⚄	Theater Stage	Rapid Relief Equipment	Loudspeakers
⚅	Fortified Command Center	Rugged Terrain Kits	Royal Sigils

	⚃	⚄	⚅
⚀	Alchemical Labs	Mounted Cannons	Cloaking Device
⚁	Hidden Compartments	Ironclad Sides	High-Definition Radars
⚂	Secure Holding Cells	Automated Turrets	Weather Instruments
⚃	Submersible Scouts	Radar Systems	Mining Lasers
⚄	Salvage Drones	Mercenary Armory	Research Modules
⚅	Massive Cargo Holds	Strategic War Room	High-Atmosphere Antennas

SHIPYARD

Here, airships of various designs and capabilities are forged, each a testament to the ingenuity of their creators. Choose your vessel wisely, for it shall be your trusted companion in the skies.

SKYSTRIDER VOYAGER
- **Concept:** Swift Explorer
- **Skills:** Aerial Navigation, Cartography
- **Frailty:** Vulnerable to Storms
- **Gear:** High-Powered Binoculars, Wind-Speed Indicator

IRONCLAD ENFORCER
- **Concept:** Aerial Warship
- **Skills:** Gunnery, Broadside Coordination
- **Frailty:** Heavy and Slow
- **Gear:** Artillery Cannons, Armor Reinforcements

WHISPERWIND COURIER
- **Concept:** Stealthy Infiltrator
- **Skills:** Invisibility Cloaking, Silent Navigation
- **Frailty:** Fragile Hull
- **Gear:** Cloaking Device, Silent Propellers

THUNDERCLAW MARAUDER
- **Concept:** Sky Pirate Raider
- **Skills:** Boarding Maneuvers, Sabotage
- **Frailty:** Limited Fuel Capacity
- **Gear:** Boarding Ramps, Fuel Siphons

CLOUDSKIMMER EXPLORER
- **Concept:** High-Altitude Surveyor
- **Skills:** Altitude Adjustment, Atmospheric Analysis
- **Frailty:** Vulnerable to Atmospheric Phenomena
- **Gear:** Altitude Control Valve, Atmospheric Sensors

CELESTIAL NAVIGATOR
- **Concept:** Long-Distance Voyager
- **Skills:** Star Navigation, Long-Range Communication
- **Frailty:** Navigational Complexity
- **Gear:** Celestial Compass, Signal Boosters

STEAMBOATS

In the world of *Cog & Compass*, steamboats are essential for navigating the myriad rivers, lakes, and coastal waters. These vessels range from rugged industrial workhorses to elegant floating palaces, each crafted to fulfill specific roles in a world dominated by steam and steel.

CONCEPTS

	⚀	⚁	⚂
⚀	River Trader	Coastal Freighter	Pleasure Cruiser
⚁	Fishing Trawler	Luxury Yacht	Scientific Surveyor
⚂	Ore Transport	River Casino	Weather Ship
⚃	Whaling Ship	Diplomatic Envoy	Underwater Salvager
⚄	Amphibious Carrier	Cultural Gallery	Stealth Recon
⚅	Armored Warship	Royal Barge	Myth Hunter

	⚃	⚄	⚅
⚀	Industrial Tug	Exploration Vessel	Smuggler's Runner
⚁	Icebreaker	Patrol Boat	Floating Market
⚂	Naval Gunboat	Research Platform	Refugee Carrier
⚃	Hospital Ship	Pirate Skiff	Hydroplant
⚄	Prison Barge	Treasure Hunter	Disaster Relief
⚅	Deep Sea Miner	Rebel Base	Mobile Fortress

SKILLS

	⚀	⚁	⚂
⚀	Efficient Navigation	Coastal Mastery	Entertainment Facilities
⚁	Deep Sea Fishing	Opulent Comfort	Environmental Monitoring
⚂	Bulk Cargo Handling	Gambling Systems	Meteorological Equipment
⚃	Whaling Harpoons	Diplomatic Facilities	Salvage Operations
⚄	Amphibious Operation	Art Exhibits	Silent Running
⚅	Fortified Hull	Royal Quarters	Mythical Equipment

	⚃	⚄	⚅
⚀	Heavy Lifting	Advanced Sonar	Stealth Navigation
⚁	Ice Navigation	Rapid Response	Vendor Stalls
⚂	Cannonade	Submersible Support	Emergency Housing
⚃	Medical Facilities	Boarding Tactics	Power Generation
⚄	Detainee Containment	Artifact Retrieval	Rescue Equipment
⚅	Drilling Rigs	Covert Operations	Siege Weapons

FRAILTIES

	⚀	⚁	⚂
⚀	Prone to Silting	Hull Corrosion	High Maintenance
⚁	Fuel Hog	Overly Luxurious	Sensitive Instruments
⚂	Heavy Draft	Gambling Debts	Weather Dependent
⚃	Old Equipment	Political Target	Salvage Malfunctions
⚄	Low Bridge Clearance	Cultural Clashes	Noise Pollution
⚅	High Profile	Royal Scrutiny	Creature Attraction

	⚃	⚄	⚅
⚀	Slow Speed	Radar Signature	Lightly Armored
⚁	Vulnerable to Ice	Limited Weaponry	Crowded Deck
⚂	Target for Pirates	Submersible Risk	Insufficient Lifeboats
⚃	Contagion Risk	Easy to Board	Power Drain
⚄	Fire Risk	Treasure Obsession	Rescue Delays
⚅	Depth Limited	Rebel Target	Bombardment Risk

GEAR

	⚀	⚁	⚂
⚀	Advanced Maps	Stabilized Hull	Theater Systems
⚁	Fishing Nets	Plush Furnishings	Environmental Sensors
⚂	Ore Bins	Roulette Wheels	Weather Stations
⚃	Harpoon Launchers	Embassy Suites	Diving Gear
⚄	All-Terrain Treads	Art Galleries	Noise Suppressors
⚅	Reinforced Armor	Opulent Quarters	Mythical Relics

	⚃	⚄	⚅
⚀	Industrial Cranes	Depth Sounders	Cloaking Screens
⚁	Icebreaker Bow	Water Cannons	Floating Stalls
⚂	Mounted Guns	Research Labs	Compact Housing
⚃	Hospital Wards	Grappling Hooks	Turbines
⚄	Prison Cells	Treasure Scopes	Emergency Kits
⚅	Mining Dredges	Hidden Compartments	Heavy Artillery

SHIPYARD

At the shipyard, steamboats of diverse designs and capabilities are meticulously crafted, each a testament to the ingenuity of their creators. Choose your vessel wisely, for it shall be your trusted companion on the waterways.

RIVER RUNNER
- **Concept:** Agile Transport
- **Skills:** River Navigation, Rapid Maneuvering
- **Frailty:** Shallow Draft Limitations
- **Gear:** Retractable Keel, Streamlined Hull

IRONCLAD LEVIATHAN
- **Concept:** Armored Warship
- **Skills:** Heavy Gunnery, Armor Plating Mastery
- **Frailty:** Cumbersome Handling
- **Gear:** Reinforced Bulkheads, Cannon Arrays

MISTY MERCHANT
- **Concept:** Covert Smuggler
- **Skills:** Stealth Transport, Silent Running
- **Frailty:** Limited Cargo Space
- **Gear:** Concealed Compartments, Noise Reduction Propellers

GALE RIDER
- **Concept:** Storm Navigator
- **Skills:** Storm Endurance, High-Speed Steering
- **Frailty:** Prone to Overturning
- **Gear:** Storm Anchors, High-Torque Rudders

DELTA EXPLORER
- **Concept:** Versatile Surveyor
- **Skills:** Multi-environment Navigation, Ecological Sampling
- **Frailty:** Sensitive Instruments
- **Gear:** Multi-depth Sonar, Environmental Labs

SOVEREIGN AMBASSADOR
- **Concept:** Diplomatic Envoy
- **Skills:** International Waters Navigation, Diplomatic Entertaining
- **Frailty:** High-Value Target
- **Gear:** Luxurious Suites, Secure Communication Systems

LAND VEHICLES

These marvels of engineering meld period-appropriate technology with inventive flair to offer a variety of transportation and utility solutions suited to the diverse needs of the realm.

IRON SERPENTS (IRON SERPENTS)

Concept: Massive, multi-carriage vehicles powered by steam engines, designed to traverse extensive land routes. These "land trains" or "iron serpents" could follow set tracks or be equipped with large, rugged wheels suitable for open terrain.

Common Uses: - Freight and Cargo Transport: Moving goods across vast continents where railway infrastructure may be lacking or damaged. - Passenger Travel: Offering a more scenic and leisurely travel option compared to rapid air travel, accommodating passengers in comfort akin to the luxury of great ocean liners.

STEAM-POWERED WAGONS (AUTOMOBILES)

Concept: Smaller, more maneuverable steam-powered wagons or automobiles, suitable for individual or small group travel. These vehicles are akin to the early cars of the late 19th century but powered by compact steam engines.

Common Uses: - Personal Transportation: For the affluent classes, providing a private and flexible way to travel. - Urban Cabs: Serving as taxis in larger metropolitan areas, steam cabs would be a common sight, whisking passengers through bustling city streets.

MECHANICAL WALKERS (STEAM MECHS)

Concept: Large, bipedal or multi-pedal machines powered by steam and intricate clockwork mechanisms. These could range from utilitarian designs used in construction and heavy industry to more militaristic models outfitted for patrol or combat in unstable regions.

Common Uses: - Industrial Work: Performing laborious tasks in environments too hazardous for human workers, such as mining, logging, or construction in treacherous areas. - Military Applications: Patrolling borders or being involved in skirmishes where their imposing presence and capability to traverse difficult terrains are advantageous.

STEAM CRAWLERS (EXPLORATION ROVERS)

Concept: Robust, all-terrain vehicles designed for exploration, equipped with features like steam-powered drills, cranes, and other apparatus for scientific and exploratory missions in uncharted territories.

Common Uses: - Geographical Surveys: Charting new lands, collecting geological samples, and mapping out natural resources. - Archaeological Expeditions: Transporting teams to dig sites and providing on-site processing power.

LUXURY ROAD COACHES

Concept: Elegant, long-distance coaches providing high comfort and amenities, powered by steam engines, and designed for the leisurely travel of the elite, reminiscent of the grand rail experiences but on rubberized or metallic wheels.

Common Uses: - Leisure Travel: Offering luxury tours through scenic and culturally rich routes. - Diplomatic Missions: Transporting dignitaries and officials on state visits in style and comfort.

GARAGE

Each of these vehicles highlights the innovative integration of steam power into different aspects of transportation and work within a steampunk world, showcasing their unique capabilities and limitations.

IRON SERPENT

- **Concept:** Continental Freighter
- **Skills:** Long-Distance Hauling, Heavy Load Management
- **Frailty:** Requires Constant Track Maintenance
- **Gear:** Modular Cargo Carriages, Reinforced Engine Components

STEAM CARRIAGE

- **Concept:** Urban Commuter
- **Skills:** Agile Navigation, Efficient Fuel Consumption
- **Frailty:** Limited Range
- **Gear:** Compact Steam Engine, Pneumatic Suspension

STEAM MECH

- **Concept:** Industrial Titan
- **Skills:** Heavy Lifting, Precision Placement
- **Frailty:** High Fuel Consumption
- **Gear:** Hydraulic Arms, All-Terrain Legs

STEAM CRAWLER

- **Concept:** Arctic Explorer
- **Skills:** All-Weather Operation, Ice Navigation
- **Frailty:** Vulnerable to Extreme Cold
- **Gear:** Thermal Insulation, Ice-Melting Equipment

ROAD COACH

- **Concept:** Luxury Tourer
- **Skills:** Smooth Ride, Guest Entertainment
- **Frailty:** High Maintenance Costs
- **Gear:** Ornate Interior, Advanced Suspension System

EXPLORING THE WORLD

Cog & Compass throws you headfirst into the exploration of a fantastical world powered by steam and clockwork. Whether you navigate by airship, steamboat, or land vehicle, these exploration rules will guide you through uncharted territories and thrilling encounters.

PREPARATION

- **Define Your Destination:** Choose a specific location on your map (hand-drawn or provided) or have the Oracle (dice rolls) determine a general direction and a rumor about a point of interest.
- **Choose Your Mode of Travel:** Consider your character's skills, resources, and the desired speed of travel. Airships are fast but vulnerable to storms, steamboats are excellent for rivers and coasts but slow, and land vehicles offer flexibility but encounter rough terrain challenges.
- **Stock Up:** Gather supplies based on your chosen travel time and potential hazards (coal for steamboats, spare parts for airships, food and water for all).

THE JOURNEY

A. AIRSHIP EXPLORATION

- **Navigation Check:** Roll a d6 to navigate. On a 4+, navigate successfully. On a 3 or less, consult the "Airship Encounters" table for a random encounter or complication.
- **Weather Check:** Every d6 hours roll a d6. On a 1 or 2, encounter rough weather (strong winds, lightning storms) that may damage your airship (apply a relevant trait to the airship).
- **Scouting Check (optional):** Attempt to scout the landing area. Before landing in an unexplored area, roll a d6. On a 4+, gain a brief glimpse of the surrounding terrain and potential dangers. On a 3 or less, you miss crucial details.

B. STEAMBOAT EXPLORATION

- **Navigation Check:** Roll a d6 to navigate. On a 4+, navigate successfully. On a 3 or less, consult the "Steambot Encounters" table for a random encounter or complication.
- **Current Check:** Every d6 hours, roll a d6. On a 1 or 2, encounter strong currents or hazardous rapids that may require skillful maneuvering to avoid damage.
- **River Ambush Check:** On rivers with a reputation for piracy, roll a d6 after each successful navigation check. On a 1 or 2, encounter river pirates demanding a toll or initiating a combat encounter.

C. LAND VEHICLE EXPLORATION

- **Navigation Check (d6):** Roll a d6 to navigate. On a 4+, navigate successfully. On a 3 or less, consult the "Land Encounters" table for a random encounter or complication.
- **Terrain Check (d6):** Every d6 hours, roll a d6. On a 1 or 2, encounter difficult terrain (steep hills, dense forests) that slows your progress (reduce travel speed by half).
- **Ambush Check (d6):** In bandit-ridden areas, roll a d6 after each successful navigation check. On a 1 or 2, encounter bandits demanding valuables or initiating a combat encounter.

REACHING YOUR DESTINATION

Upon reaching your destination, consult your map or the Oracle for details about the location and potential encounters. This could be a bustling city, a forgotten ruin, a hidden valley inhabited by strange creatures, or anything your imagination conjures. Use your character's skills and the exploration mechanics to overcome challenges, gather information, and uncover the secrets of the Cog & Compass Era.

URBAN ADVENTURES

The smog-choked cities of the Cog & Compass Era are teeming with life, opportunity, and danger. Here's how your character can interact with these urban environments.

Remember: The urban environment is full of potential allies and adversaries. Use your character's skills, negotiate deals, and overcome challenges to navigate the complex web of the *Cog & Compass* city.

GATHER INFORMATION

- **Talk to the Townsfolk:** Mingle with shopkeepers, bartenders, or laborers in taverns and marketplaces (roll a conflict for guarded information).
- **Consult the Cog & Compass Gazette:** This ubiquitous newspaper provides news, rumors, and classifieds (success determined by the information's rarity).
- **Visit the Clockwork Library:** A vast repository of knowledge, but accessing restricted sections may require a disguise (roll a conflict for guards) or a successful bribery attempt (roll a conflict for librarian).

ACQUIRE GOODS AND SERVICES

- **Shop at Tinkerers' Guild:** Find the latest gadgets, clockwork contraptions, and spare parts (price and availability determined by the item's rarity).
- **Hire Specialists:** Blacksmiths can repair your vehicle, doctors can heal wounds, and inventors can create custom contraptions (cost based on service and complexity).
- **Haggle at the Marketplace:** Find a diverse range of goods, from exotic spices to salvaged machinery (roll a conflict for best price).

UNDERTAKE DARING MISSIONS

- **Infiltrate a Factory:** Investigate unsafe working conditions or uncover a secret project (roll a conflict for guards, success unlocks further exploration).
- **Steal Classified Documents:** Break into a wealthy industrialist's mansion or a government office (roll a conflict for security measures, success grants access to documents).
- **Help the Smogbreakers:** Assist a clandestine group fighting for environmental reform by sabotaging polluting factories (roll a conflict for guards, success hinders factory output).

FACE URBAN CHALLENGES

- **Navigate the Crowds:** Hustle through bustling market-places or escape pursuing guards through narrow alleys (roll a conflict for agility).
- **Chase a Pickpocket:** Pursue a nimble thief through the city's rooftops or crowded streets (roll a conflict for dexterity).
- **Bar Brawl in a Tavern:** Defend yourself or a friend from drunken thugs (roll a conflict for combat prowess).

SETTING INFORMATION

ECONOMIC DYNAMICS AND RESOURCES IN THE COG & COMPASS ERA

THE BLACK GOLD RUSH:
- **Coal:** The lifeblood of the Cog & Compass Era. Nations with rich coal deposits wield immense power.
- **Coal Wars:**
  - **Resource Scarcity:** Friction is inevitable as easily accessible coal reserves dwindle. Border skirmishes, espionage, and proxy wars erupt over control of new mines and transportation routes.
  - **The "Black Barons":** Ruthless industrialists control vast coal mines, amassing immense wealth and political influence. Workers in these mines toil in harsh conditions, fueling labor unrest and potential revolutions.
- **Alternative Fuels:** Research into alternative fuels like compressed natural gas or even rudimentary geothermal energy is underway, but coal remains king for now.

THE POWER OF INVENTION:
- **Steam Rights & Patents:**
  - **Patent Wars:** A fierce competition rages among inventors and corporations to secure patents on groundbreaking steam technologies. Legal battles and corporate espionage are commonplace, with fortunes won and lost on the drafting table.
  - **The Guilds of Steam:** Prestigious organizations like the British Royal Society of Steam Engineers and the American Guild of Automata Artisans control access to knowledge and training. Membership grants prestige and lucrative contracts, but can also be exclusionary and stifle innovation from outside sources.
  - **Black Markets:** A thriving black market exists for stolen schematics and prototype automata, catering to nations and corporations desperate to catch up in the technological race.

BEYOND COAL:

- **Strategic Resources:** Other resources like iron, copper, and rubber are crucial for building and maintaining steam technology. Nations with access to these resources hold a strategic advantage.
- **The Rise of Resource Cartels:** Powerful consortia of nations and corporations might form to control the flow of vital resources, manipulating prices and influencing global politics.
- **Exploration & Exploitation:** The "Age of Exploration" has a new agenda: the discovery of new resource-rich territories. Colonial powers race to claim uncharted lands, often at the expense of the indigenous populations. Exploration companies funded by resource-hungry nations push the boundaries of the known world.

CULTURAL FLOURISHING IN THE COG & COMPASS ERA:

FASHION & SOCIAL ETIQUETTE:

- **Gear & Glory:** Steampunk aesthetics permeate everyday life. Clothing incorporates brass buttons, gear shaped patterns, and leather accents. Goggles are not just for pilots, but a common fashion statement for the discerning citizen.
- **Automata Companions:** The display and maintenance of personal automata becomes a mark of social status. The wealthy flaunt their intricately crafted companions, while etiquette dictates proper interaction with these mechanical marvels.
- **Bespoke Enhancements:** The truly affluent indulge in personalized steam-powered accessories. Pocket calculators for the businessman, parasols that unfurl with the whir of gears for the lady, or even clockwork monocles for the eccentric gentleman.

ART & LITERATURE:

- **Steam-Powered Muse:** The marvels of steam technology inspire a new artistic movement. Sculptures incorporate pistons and gears, paintings depict fantastical steam-powered cities, and clockwork contraptions create intricate patterns and automata-powered ballets.
- **The Clatter of Typewriters:** The rise of steam-powered printing presses and typewriters fuels a literary explosion. Steampunk novels filled with airships, clockwork creations, and intrepid inventors become wildly popular.

- **Interactive Experiences:** Cultural institutions embrace the power of steam. Opera houses boast elaborate moving sets powered by pistons, while art galleries showcase interactive exhibits where viewers can manipulate steam-powered sculptures.
- **The Automaton Orchestra:** Clockwork musicians take the stage, flawlessly performing classical masterpieces with an uncanny precision. Automata actors deliver Shakespearean monologues with surprising emotional nuance, blurring the lines between machine and performer.

BEYOND THE UPPER CRUST:

- **Folklore & Fear:** While the wealthy revel in steam's wonders, some regard automata with suspicion. Folklore warns of machines rising up against their creators, and some religious sects view steam technology as an affront to God.
- **The Ballad of the Cogsmith:** Street performers sing of daring inventors, tragic factory accidents, and the struggles of the working class. These ballads reflect the social anxieties and aspirations of the common people.

THE BLENDING OF TECHNOLOGY AND WONDER

SPECTACLE & DECEPTION: MECHANICAL MAGIC SHOWS:

In the absence of traditional magic, a unique form of entertainment has emerged:

- **The Steampunk Stage:** Talented inventors and illusionists combine clockwork, mirrors, and steam to create awe-inspiring spectacles. Audiences gasp as rabbits appear from seemingly empty hatboxes powered by hidden mechanisms, and levitating performers defy gravity with the aid of cleverly concealed steam-powered platforms.
- **Masters of Misdirection:** These shows are not just about entertainment. Adept performers can use their skills for more clandestine purposes. Secret compartments hidden within automatons, coded messages delivered through seemingly harmless illusions, and elaborate escapes engineered under the cover of dazzling illusions offer opportunities for espionage or rebellion.

THE BLURRING LINE: CLOCKWORK CREATURES:

The advancement of automata technology has led to the creation of a controversial class of machines:

- **Bio-mechanical Marvels:** These are creatures that blend flesh and metal. Clockwork hearts pump blood, and intricate steam engines power their movements.
- **Pets or Pariahs?:** On one hand, bio-mechanical pets are a novelty. Wealthy families might have clockwork canaries that sing elaborate melodies or robotic dogs with impressive agility. However, the ethical implications are hotly debated. Animal rights activists protest the cruelty of using living creatures in these machines, while religious leaders see them as an unnatural abomination.
- **Beasts of Burden:** Some nations explore the use of bio-mechanical creatures for military or industrial purposes. Imagine colossal clockwork horses pulling artillery wagons, or monstrous bio-mechanical bears patrolling the wilderness. The potential for these creations to become uncontrollable weapons adds another layer of tension to the international landscape.

THE PRICE OF PROGRESS: POLITICAL AND SOCIAL CHALLENGES IN THE COG & COMPASS ERA

THE AUTOMATA QUESTION

- **The Rise of Automata Rights:** As automata become more sophisticated, some begin to exhibit surprising levels of intelligence and even rudimentary emotions. This sparks the Automata Rights Movement, a growing social and political movement arguing that these advanced creations deserve rights and recognition not as machines, but as sentient beings.
- **A Spark That Could Ignite the World:** The debate surrounding automata rights is a powder keg waiting to explode. Proponents advocate for better working conditions, legal protections, and even the right of automata to choose their own destinies. Opponents fear the consequences of granting machines sentience and potential autonomy.

THE GLOBAL STEAM COUNCIL:

- **Maintaining Balance:** The rapid advancement of steam technology has spurred concerns about its destructive potential. To mitigate this, a powerful international body called the Global Steam Council has been established.

- **Composition & Goals:** Made up of representatives from all major powers, the Council aims to regulate the use of steam technology, control the proliferation of advanced weaponry, and prevent international conflicts fueled by technological superiority.

- **A Delicate Dance:** The Council navigates a complex political landscape. Espionage and sabotage are rife as each nation attempts to gain an edge. Balancing national interests with the need for global stability proves an ongoing challenge.

FACTIONS & ORGANIZATIONS

THE MECHANICAL ENGINEERS

- **Concept:** Innovative Tinkerers
- **Skills:** Steam Mechanics, Invention
- **Frailty:** Overeager Curiosity
- **Gear:** Steam Pulse Gauntlets, Clockwork Automata
- **Goal:** Unveil the Secrets of Steam Technology
- **Motive:** Advancing Technology for the Betterment of Society
- **Nemesis:** The Clockwork Syndicate

The Mechanical Engineers are a guild of brilliant minds and deft hands, dedicated to pushing the boundaries of what steam and clockwork can achieve. This group of inventors and tinkerers is driven by an insatiable curiosity and a noble mission to harness technology for the betterment of society. They are frequently seen donning steam pulse gauntlets and accompanied by intricate clockwork automata. Despite their genius, their overeager curiosity sometimes leads them into dangerous territories or moral quandaries. Their main adversaries are the Clockwork Syndicate, who covet the Engineers' creations for less altruistic purposes.

THE SMOGBREAKERS

- **Concept:** Environmental Vigilantes
- **Skills:** Smog Resistance, Sabotage
- **Frailty:** Idealistic Zeal
- **Gear:** Gas-Mask Respirators, Smog-Dissipating Bombs
- **Goal:** Cleanse the Skies from Industrial Pollution
- **Motive:** Protecting Nature and Vulnerable Populace
- **Nemesis:** The Industrial Magnates

The Smogbreakers stand as vigilant defenders of the environment amidst the smoke-choked cities of the steampunk world. These environmental vigilantes are skilled in navigating and resisting the dense industrial smog that plagues the urban landscapes. Armed with gas-mask respirators and smog-dissipating bombs, they aim to cleanse the skies and protect vulnerable communities from the suffocating grip of industrial pollution. Their zeal is fueled by a deep-seated desire to restore nature's balance, putting them at odds with the profit-driven Industrial Magnates.

THE CLOCKWORK SYNDICATE

- **Concept:** Masterful Thieves
- **Skills:** Lock-picking, Deception
- **Frailty:** Loyalty to Wealth
- **Gear:** Gear-Enhanced Lockpicks, Stealthy Goggles
- **Goal:** Acquire Priceless Technological Artifacts
- **Motive:** Amassing Wealth and Technological Superiority
- **Nemesis:** The Technological Enforcers
- The Clockwork Syndicate operates in the shadows of the bustling steampunk cities, a network of masterful thieves and cunning rogues. Specializing in the acquisition of technological artifacts, their members are experts in lock-picking and deception, equipped with gear-enhanced lockpicks and stealthy goggles. Driven by a relentless pursuit of wealth and technological superiority, they often find themselves clashing with the Technological Enforcers, who seek to uphold law and order amidst the technological chaos the Syndicate thrives in.

THE NEO-INDUSTRIAL LEAGUE

- **Concept:** High-Society Elites
- **Skills:** Social Manipulation, Etiquette
- **Frailty:** Arrogant Disregard
- **Gear:** Fine Attire, Steam-Powered Carriages
- **Goal:** Maintain Their Social Status Amidst Technological Changes
- **Motive:** Upholding Tradition and Privilege
- **Nemesis:** The Steamworker's Collective

The Neo-Industrial League represents the elite upper crust of society, where old money meets the new industrial age. These high-society elites are adept in social manipulation and maintain their grip on power through polished etiquette and lavish steam-powered carriages.

Their goal is to preserve their age-old privileges and influence amidst the rapid technological changes threatening their traditional ways of life.
The League's disdain for the lower classes stirs tension, making them natural adversaries of the Steamworker's Collective, who represent the working class's interests.

THE IRON VANGUARD
- **Concept:** Militant Inventors
- **Skills:** Steam-Powered Combat, Weaponsmithing
- **Frailty:** Impulsiveness
- **Gear:** Steam-Powered Battle Suits, Gatling Gauntlets
- **Goal:** Establish Technological Supremacy Through Force
- **Motive:** Forging a New World Order Based on Technology
- **Nemesis:** The Gearwrights' Guild

The Iron Vanguard is a formidable force in the world of steam and gear, composed of militant inventors and hardened warriors who believe in establishing order through technological supremacy. They are equipped with steam-powered battle suits and Gatling gauntlets, making them a formidable presence on any battlefield. Their impulsive strategy and aggressive tactics aim to forge a new world order dominated by those who control technology. They frequently clash with the Gearwrights' Guild, defenders of ethical engineering and technological distribution.

THE ASTRAL CARTOGRAPHERS
- **Concept:** Celestial Explorers
- **Skills:** Sky Navigation, Celestial Mapping
- **Frailty:** Obsession with the Heavens
- **Gear:** Starlight Scopes, High-Altitude Balloons
- **Goal:** Map the Uncharted Skies and Stars
- **Motive:** Exploring and Documenting the Unknown
- **Nemesis:** The Cloud Marauders

The Astral Cartographers are explorers of the celestial domain, charting the skies and the stars beyond the reach of ordinary skyfarers. Obsessed with the heavens, they employ starlight scopes and high-altitude balloons to navigate and map the unknown. Their quest for knowledge leads them to discover new realms and cosmic phenomena, driven by a profound motive to document the uncharted for future generations. However, their exploration efforts put them at odds with the Cloud Marauders, a group that seeks to exploit newly discovered territories and phenomena for their own gain.

THE GREAT POWERS OF THE COG & COMPASS ERA

The Cog & Compass Era is a time of fervent innovation and simmering international tension. Here's a detailed look at the major powers shaping this world:

THE BRITISH EMPIRE: THE IRON LEVIATHAN

- **Strengths:** Britain is the undisputed leader in automata and calculation engines. Their factories churn out clockwork marvels and sophisticated analytical devices coveted worldwide. London, shrouded in perpetual smog, is a testament to their industrial might. Towering smokestacks pierce the sky, and steam-powered carriages navigate a labyrinth of iron and glass buildings.
- **Weaknesses:** Britain's relentless focus on industrial progress has come at a cost. The working class simmers with discontent, yearning for better wages and safer working conditions. Pollution from coal-fired engines chokes the air, and whispers of revolution echo in the shadows.
- **Ambitions:** Britain seeks to maintain its global dominance by pushing the boundaries of steam technology. They constantly strive for innovative automata designs and superior calculation engines to secure their economic and military advantage.

THE GERMAN CONFEDERATION: THE GEARS OF PRECISION

- **Strengths:** Germany's meticulous engineering prowess rivals Britain's. Their steam-powered machines are renowned for their reliability and durability. From colossal steam-powered drills carving tunnels through mountains to intricate clockwork automatons performing delicate surgeries, German engineering is a force to be reckoned with.
- **Weaknesses:** Germany's rigid social hierarchy fuels resentment. The pursuit of efficiency above all else can lead to a stifling environment for innovation. Additionally, their focus on practicality sometimes comes at the expense of aesthetic appeal, which the French are quick to exploit.
- **Ambitions:** Germany aspires to surpass Britain as the world's leading industrial power. They prioritize the development of powerful steam-powered war machines and reliable infrastructure to bolster their growing military and industrial might.

THE UNITED STATES OF AMERICA: THE WILD WEST STEAMS AHEAD

- **Strengths:** The American spirit of innovation thrives in the Cog & Compass Era. With vast resources and a rapidly expanding frontier, the US utilizes steam technology to fuel its agricultural and manufacturing boom. Airships crisscross the vast plains, delivering supplies and connecting burgeoning settlements. Cities like New York and Chicago are bustling hubs of steam-powered invention and entrepreneurial spirit.
- **Weaknesses:** Rapid growth creates social unrest. The influx of immigrants and the exploitation of natural resources lead to tensions. Tensions simmer between the wealthy industrialists on the East Coast and the frontier communities carving a life out West.
- **Ambitions:** The US dreams of becoming a self-sufficient industrial powerhouse. They actively seek technological advancements to improve agriculture, transportation, and communication, ultimately aiming to surpass the established powers of Europe.

THE FRENCH REPUBLIC: ART & ELEGANCE POWERED BY STEAM

- **Strengths:** France prioritizes aesthetics and cultural refinement in its use of steam technology. Parisian boulevards are adorned with steam-powered streetlights, and grand opera houses boast elaborate sets powered by pistons and gears. French automata are renowned for their intricate clockwork and lifelike movements.
- **Weaknesses:** France's focus on style can sometimes come at the expense of practicality. Their automata, while stunning, may not be as robust as their British or German counterparts. Additionally, political instability can hinder their ability to compete in the global industrial race.
- **Ambitions:** France desires to maintain its cultural influence in the face of growing industrialization. They strive to showcase the beauty and elegance of steam technology, hoping to set the global standard for aesthetics in the new era.

THE JAPANESE EMPIRE: TRADITION MEETS INNOVATION

- **Strengths:** Japan's unique blend of tradition and steam technology sets them apart. Samurai warriors clad in steam-powered armor wield fearsome clockwork weaponry, seamlessly integrating ancient traditions with the marvels of the Cog & Compass Era. Their steam-powered locomotives navigate treacherous mountain passes, showcasing their ability to adapt technology to their specific needs.
- **Weaknesses:** Japan is a newcomer to the international stage. Their industrial base is not yet on par with the European powers, and their resources are limited. Additionally, their insular culture can sometimes hinder technological exchange and collaboration.
- **Ambitions:** Japan seeks to carve its niche in the new world order. They strive to modernize their military and industry while preserving their cultural heritage. They hope to earn the respect of the established powers through their unique approach to steam technology.

THE TSARIST EMPIRE: THE COLOSSUS OF STEAM

- **Strengths:** Ruled by an iron fist, the Tsarist Empire commands vast resources. They are willing to pour immense manpower and materials into research and development, focusing on brute force and size when it comes to automata and airships. Their sheer scale and willingness to utilize unconventional methods can be a concern for other nations.
- **Weaknesses:** Despite their vast resources, the Tsarist Empire suffers from inefficiency and corruption. The harsh central control stifles innovation, and funds often get siphoned off before reaching research projects. Additionally, their reliance on brute force can lead to cumbersome and unreliable machinery compared to the more elegant designs of other nations.
- **Ambitions:** The Tsars dream of regaining their lost prestige and becoming a dominant power on the world stage. They see steam technology as a tool to modernize their military, expand their borders, and force other nations to recognize their might. However, their ambitions are often hampered by internal dissent and a growing technological gap separating them from the leading industrial powers.

INTERNATIONAL RELATIONS AND TECHNOLOGICAL ESPIONAGE

The Cog & Compass Era is a time of uneasy alliances and simmering tensions. Here's a glimpse into the complex web of international relations and the shadow world of technological espionage:

- **The Global Steam Council:** A fragile alliance exists between the major powers in the form of the Global Steam Council. Formed to prevent open warfare and regulate the use of steam technology, the council serves as a forum for diplomacy and (often) thinly veiled threats. Each nation has a representative, but tensions are high as accusations of espionage and sabotage fly.
- **The Whispers of War:** Beneath the surface of diplomacy, a shadow war rages. Each nation employs a network of spies and informants to steal technological secrets and sabotage their rivals' progress. The theft of blueprints, the infiltration of research facilities, and the manipulation of international incidents are all tools employed in this clandestine struggle.
- Friction Points:
  - **British Colonial Ambitions:** Britain's relentless expansionism creates resentment among indigenous populations and rising powers like Japan.
  - **The Franco-German Rivalry:** A long history of animosity fuels the competition between France and Germany, spilling over into the race for technological dominance.
  - **The American Challenge:** The rapid rise of the United States as an industrial power disrupts the established order, creating anxiety among the European powers.
- **The Rise of Neutrality:** Smaller nations, caught in the crossfire between the superpowers, are increasingly seeking to maintain neutrality. They may play the major powers against each other to secure favorable trade deals or avoid being drawn into a potential war.
- **The Threat of Radicalism:** The rise of labor unrest and the spread of radical ideologies pose a potential threat to the established order. Some radical groups view steam technology as a tool of oppression, while others advocate for its use to overthrow the existing power structures. These movements are closely monitored by the governments of the major powers, fearing revolution or acts of sabotage.

- **Technological Espionage:**
  - **The Gearhounds:** A loose network of skilled thieves and smugglers specialize in stealing valuable technological blueprints and prototypes. They operate across borders, offering their services to the highest bidder, be it a nation-state or a wealthy industrialist.
  - **The Ministry of Patent Enforcement:** This international body seeks to prevent the illegal trade of stolen technology. Operating with limited resources and often hampered by national interests, they struggle to keep up with the Gearhounds' agility.

THE GREAT POWERS AND THE FACTIONS: A TANGLED WEB

The rise of steam technology creates new opportunities and challenges for both the established powers and the various factions within the Cog & Compass Era. Here's how they might interact:

THE BRITISH EMPIRE

- **The Mechanical Engineers:** The British government may sponsor the Engineers' research, hoping for breakthroughs that could strengthen their military and industrial might. However, they may also be wary of the Engineers' tendency to share their inventions freely, potentially upsetting the balance of power.
- **The Smogbreakers:** The British government is likely to be conflicted about the Smogbreakers. While they acknowledge the environmental damage caused by industry, they also fear the Smogbreakers' radical tactics could disrupt production and hurt the economy.
- **The Clockwork Syndicate:** Britain will dedicate significant resources to tracking down the Syndicate, especially if they target critical technological secrets. They might even employ their own network of spies to infiltrate the Syndicate and disrupt their operations.
- **The Neo-Industrial League:** The British government relies on the League's financial backing and influence to maintain its global standing. However, the League's resistance to worker reforms could lead to social unrest, which the government would have to address.
- **The Iron Vanguard:** Britain views the Vanguard with suspicion, fearing their aggressive expansionist goals. They might try to manipulate other powers to contain the Vanguard's influence.
- **The Astral Cartographers:** The British government is likely to sponsor the Cartographers' expeditions, seeking to map new trade routes and discover potential resources beyond their current reach.

THE GERMAN CONFEDERATION

- **The Mechanical Engineers:** Germany welcomes the Engineers' innovative spirit and may offer them funding and resources in exchange for exclusive access to their inventions. However, they may also be concerned about potential leaks of technology to rival nations.
- **The Smogbreakers:** The German government shares Britain's concerns about the Smogbreakers' disruptive tactics. However, they may be more receptive to their environmental message if it can be presented in a way that doesn't threaten industrial output.
- **The Clockwork Syndicate:** Germany, like Britain, will dedicate resources to stopping the Syndicate from acquiring their technology. They may even collaborate with other powers on this front.
- **The Neo-Industrial League:** Germany enjoys a good relationship with the League, as their shared focus on efficiency and order aligns their interests.
- **The Iron Vanguard:** Germany sees the Vanguard as a potential threat to their own military ambitions. They may engage in a technological arms race with the Vanguard, pushing the boundaries of steam-powered weaponry.
- **The Astral Cartographers:** Germany might offer support to the Cartographers, hoping to gain access to their discoveries and potentially use them for strategic advantage.

THE UNITED STATES OF AMERICA

- **The Mechanical Engineers:** The US government is likely to be a strong supporter of the Engineers, encouraging innovation and technological progress that fuels American expansion.
- **The Smogbreakers:** The US, with its vast frontier and focus on environmental preservation, might be more sympathetic to the Smogbreakers' cause. However, the concerns of industrialists in the East Coast cities could create internal conflict.
- **The Clockwork Syndicate:** The US will likely be targeted by the Syndicate, as their rapidly growing industrial base holds valuable technological secrets.
- **The Neo-Industrial League:** The US might have a more contentious relationship with the League, as the American spirit of self-reliance clashes with the League's established social hierarchy.
- **The Iron Vanguard:** The US views the Vanguard with a mix of caution and admiration. They may adopt some of the Vanguard's technological advancements while remaining wary of their aggressive tendencies.

- **The Astral Cartographers:** The US government is likely to sponsor American explorers and inventors collaborating with the Cartographers, eager to explore the vast potential of the uncharted territories.

THE FRENCH REPUBLIC

- **The Mechanical Engineers:** France admires the Engineers' ingenuity but may be more interested in aesthetics than pure functionality. They might collaborate on projects that combine technological innovation with artistic flair, creating elegant and stylish automata or steam-powered marvels for public entertainment.
- **The Smogbreakers:** While France values beauty, they are not blind to the environmental consequences of progress. They might offer the Smogbreakers a platform to raise awareness and advocate for cleaner technologies, perhaps through artistic campaigns or innovative pollution filters with a touch of French elegance.
- **The Clockwork Syndicate:** France, with its focus on luxury goods, could be a target for the Syndicate's more opulent and artistic creations. The Syndicate might attempt to steal or replicate intricate clockwork sculptures, automata adorned with precious jewels, or even blueprints for luxurious steam-powered carriages.
- **The Neo-Industrial League:** France shares some of the League's cultural values but may be more open to social reforms, especially those that enhance the lives of the working class. They might find themselves caught between the League's desire for social order and the growing demands for workers' rights.
- **The Iron Vanguard:** France views the Vanguard with disdain, finding their militaristic approach distasteful. The French might use diplomacy and cultural influence to counter the Vanguard's aggressive tactics.
- **The Astral Cartographers:** France, with its rich history of exploration and scientific curiosity, might sponsor French cartographers to collaborate with the international effort. They might be particularly interested in the artistic potential of celestial mapping, seeking to capture the beauty of the cosmos through their unique lens.

CITY DISTRICT ENCOUNTERS

D66	City District Encounter
11	**Industrial District:** Assist workers in a strike against factory owners.
12	**Noble Quarter:** Attend an extravagant masquerade hosted by aristocrats.
13	**Artisan Alley:** Help a struggling inventor showcase their latest creation.
14	**Waterfront Docks:** Investigate smuggling activities along the docks.
15	**Market Square:** Uncover a black market selling illegal technological artifacts.
16	**Techno-Carnival:** Participate in a contest of technological prowess.
21	**Scholar's Enclave:** Solve a puzzle in a hidden library of forgotten lore.
22	**Theater District:** Investigate the disappearance of a famous playwright.
23	**Sewer Depths:** Confront a faction of rebels hiding in the city's underbelly.
24	**Observatory:** Decode mysterious signals from distant weather balloons.
25	**Cathedral District:** Unravel a conspiracy to overthrow the city's leadership.
26	**Clockwork Plaza:** Defend against a malfunctioning automaton rampage.

D66	City District Encounter
31	**Pleasure Gardens:** Encounter a secret society in pursuit of hedonistic thrills.
32	**Engineer's Quarter:** Solve a mechanical mystery causing strange malfunctions.
33	**Refugee Camp:** Aid refugees seeking shelter from the ravages of industry.
34	**Underground Network:** Infiltrate a hidden resistance against the ruling class.
35	**Scholarly Debate:** Mediate a heated discussion among renowned academics.
36	**Smoggy Alleyways:** Navigate a labyrinthine maze of smog-choked streets.
41	**Sporting Arena:** Compete in a high-stakes mechanized gladiator match.
42	**Theater of Inventions:** Resolve technical malfunctions disrupting performances.
43	**Potion Peddler's Row:** Uncover an illicit operation distributing dangerous chemicals.
44	**Abandoned Factory:** Confront a rogue automaton wreaking havoc.
45	**Historian's Guild:** Decode a cryptic document that foretells a potential disaster.
46	**Engineer's Workshop:** Prevent a disgruntled inventor from unleashing a dangerous device.

D66	City District Encounter
51	**Garden Conservatory:** Investigate the theft of rare and exotic mechanical plants.
52	**Skybridge Heist:** Chase down a thief across the precarious city skybridges.
53	**Smuggler's Hideout:** Infiltrate a den of smugglers trafficking illegal machine parts.
54	**Clockwork Parade:** Protect the city's grand clockwork parade from sabotage.
55	**Architect's Retreat:** Seek solutions from master builders hidden within an ancient structure.
56	**The Abandoned Spire:** Ascend a forgotten tower with industrial secrets waiting to be uncovered.
61	**Guild Hall Challenge:** Compete in a contest to prove mastery in a guild's craft.
62	**Haunted Machine Shop:** Confront the mechanical remnants of the city's industrial accidents.
63	**Inventor's Convention:** Present your own creation among a host of inventors.
64	**Towering Factory:** Infiltrate an oppressive factory overseen by tyrannical managers.
65	**Veiled Auction:** Bid on rare mechanical artifacts in a shadowy auction house.
66	**Steamway Pursuit:** Chase down thieves through the city's elaborate steamway system.

URBAN LEGENDS OR RUMORS

D66	Rumor
11	Beneath the city, the Whispering Vault is rumored to hold the Mechanical Engineers' most precious inventions.
12	A hidden network of pneumatic tunnels reportedly connects the city's districts, used only by the Clockwork Syndicate.
13	There are whispers that the Clockwork Syndicate plans to pilfer the Mechanical Crown, a symbol of engineering supremacy.
14	During fierce thunderstorms, an eerie airship is said to roam the skies, piloted by a ghostly automaton.
15	Legends tell of the Nomads of the North holding a map that leads to the ancient, mythical City of Gears.
16	The Iron Vanguard's leader is said to wield a colossal steam hammer capable of leveling buildings with a single strike.
21	Deep within the Catacombs lies an ancient, enigmatic device, believed to be the first steam engine ever built.
22	The Neo-Industrial League is accused of vanishing workers who oppose their harsh labor policies.
23	In the cathedral district, a cursed automaton is rumored to bring misfortune to those who gaze upon it.
24	The Smogbreakers allegedly know the secret location of a powerful steam engine lost since the Steam Wars.
25	Hidden beneath the Clockwork Citadel is a library containing blueprints of forgotten steam-powered marvels.
26	Sewer legends speak of a mechanical kraken, said to have been built by a mad engineer banished from the city.

D66	Rumor
31	Sky pirates are rumored to navigate by a secret map leading to the legendary Sky Pirate's Cove, a haven of riches.
32	The annual Technological Inventions Exhibition is suspected to be a cover for trading corporate secrets.
33	The iron statues in the garden conservatory reportedly move under the light of the full moon, guarding ancient secrets.
34	The abandoned factory is rumored to be haunted by the spirit of an inventor who met a mysterious end.
35	An underground movement aims to overthrow the technocratic rule of the Neo-Industrial League.
36	In the engineer's quarter, a blueprint for a machine reputed to grant eternal youth is said to be hidden.
41	A hidden compartment in the Theater District's grand chandelier is rumored to hold a rare technological blueprint.
42	The Mystic Scholars claim their complex calculations can predict the rise and fall of steam-powered civilizations.
43	A legendary airship captain, known as the Storm Navigator, is said to have the ability to command the winds.
44	The Waterfront Docks are protected by a submerged ironclad, the creation of a reclusive and possibly insane inventor.
45	Tossing a special coin into the Clockwork Plaza fountain is rumored to activate an ancient mechanical underground passage.
46	Merchants in the Ironclad Bazaar are whispered to trade in rare artifacts stolen from the Mechanical Engineers.

D66	Rumor
51	Hidden beneath the city, a lost prototype of an extensive mechanical transportation system is rumored to exist.
52	The Cathedral District's bishop is said to influence his congregation with a mysterious clockwork amulet.
53	The echoes of a tragic love story are rumored to haunt the pleasure gardens at night.
54	The Technomancers' Guild has reportedly unlocked a method to revive long-dormant machines to life.
55	A complex mechanical puzzle, designed by the city's founder, supposedly guards a vault containing untold riches.
56	An airship constructed from nearly invisible materials is said to be a test vehicle escaped from a secret military project.
61	The highest spire in the city is rumored to be a portal to a lost realm floating high above the clouds.
62	The Clockwork Syndicate is believed to have acquired designs for a war automaton that could devastate armies.
63	A hidden arsenal of steam-powered weapons from an ancient conflict is said to lie forgotten in the Industrial District.
64	At the Techno-Carnival, a mechanical oracle reputedly predicts the next big advancements in steam technology with eerie accuracy.
65	The Abandoned Spire is rumored to house experimental energy sources that could revolutionize steam power.
66	A covert alliance is desperately seeking the mythical Weather Key, a device said to control the climate itself.

RANDOM EVENTS

D66	Event
11	A massive airship race is announced, attracting daring pilots from all over the world.
12	A sudden smogstorm engulfs the city, causing chaos and hampering visibility for everyone.
13	A group of workers discover a hidden chamber beneath Clockwork Citadel, revealing ancient mechanical blueprints.
14	The Neo-Aristocracy League hosts an extravagant masquerade ball, with social intrigue and hidden agendas.
15	A malfunctioning automaton wreaks havoc at the Mechanical Foundry, causing chaos among the engineers.
16	A rare celestial event bathes the skies in unusual light, sparking rumors of impending change.
21	The Iron Vanguard launches an all-out assault on a remote settlement, threatening to claim it for themselves.
22	A new type of steam-powered transportation is unveiled, promising to revolutionize travel across the skies.
23	A strange illness spreads among the population, attributed to pollution and poor working conditions.
24	A grand technology exhibition is held, showcasing the latest inventions from all the major factions.
25	A powerful mechanical device is stolen from the Technological Nexus, setting off a series of recovery efforts.
26	An underground resistance movement emerges, seeking to overthrow the ruling technocrats and establish equality.

D66	Event
31	Mechanical creatures start behaving erratically, causing disturbances across the land and skies.
32	Clockwork automatons across the city inexplicably malfunction, leading to chaos and confusion.
33	The skies open up, revealing a previously hidden floating island that holds secrets from the past.
34	A mechanical monstrosity created by the Iron Vanguard goes on a rampage, threatening the city's safety.
35	The Engineers of the Mechanical Foundry claim to have harnessed steam energy to heal injuries.
36	The Astral Cartographers discover an anomaly in the sky that may lead to an uncharted realm.
41	A series of unexplained explosions rock the Ironclad Bazaar, leading to suspicions of sabotage.
42	The Smogbreakers uncover a conspiracy to control the city's smog levels for political gain.
43	The Clockwork Syndicate recruits the protagonists for a heist targeting a high-security government facility.
44	A rare mineral is discovered deep within the city, sparking a rush of prospectors and adventurers.
45	An uprising of disgruntled steamworkers threatens to destabilize the Clockwork Citadel's ruling council.
46	A powerful storm disrupts the skies, grounding airships and causing mayhem among the skyfaring factions.

D66	Event
51	The Neo-Industrial League plans an expedition to claim forgotten technology hidden within a dangerous ruin.
52	Unpredictable steam phenomena cause chaotic effects on technology, leading to widespread disruption.
53	A charismatic leader preaches the dawn of a new technological era, gaining a significant following among the populace.
54	A mysterious figure known as the "Mechanical Phantom" starts sabotaging important technological installations.
55	The Iron Vanguard lays siege to a key strategic location, attempting to solidify their dominance in the region.
56	The protagonist receives a coded message that leads them to a hidden underground resistance against the factions.
61	A valuable mechanical core is stolen from the Technological Nexus, threatening to destabilize city operations.
62	The Clockwork Citadel's Council of Engineers unveils a revolutionary technology that could reshape societal dynamics.
63	A series of mysterious disappearances occur in the Ironclad Bazaar, pointing towards a sinister conspiracy.
64	The Smogbreakers discover a hidden underground network of tunnels that could hold the key to their cause.
65	Clockwork automatons suddenly gain self-awareness and start acting autonomously, challenging the nature of their existence.
66	A catastrophic explosion rocks the Mechanical Foundry, causing widespread damage and disrupting industrial operations.

AIRSHIP ENCOUNTERS

D66	Airship Encounter
11	**Aerial Battle:** Witness a clash between rival airship fleets.
12	**Sky Pirates:** Encounter a crew of ruthless sky pirates attempting a raid.
13	**Weather Front:** Navigate through a treacherous storm.
14	**Stowaway:** Discover an unexpected passenger hiding aboard the airship.
15	**Engine Malfunction:** The airship's engines sputter, causing turbulence.
16	**Celestial Phenomenon:** Witness a breathtaking display of natural lights.
21	**Skyward Obstacle:** Navigate around a floating island or massive cloud.
22	**Lost Airship:** Encounter a damaged airship drifting aimlessly.
23	**Airborne Market:** Stumble upon a floating bazaar of traders and merchants.
24	**Aerial Espionage:** Uncover a plot involving spies on a neighboring airship.
25	**Mechanical Failure:** Help a stranded airship crew repair their vessel.
26	**Skyward Herd:** Avoid a flock of migratory flying creatures.

D66	Airship Encounter
31	**Cloudship Nomads:** Meet a group of nomads who live aboard cloudships.
32	**Skyport Landing:** Dock at a bustling airship port, encountering customs officials and traders.
33	**Resonance Flare:** Experience a surge in steam power due to a rare atmospheric condition.
34	**Aerial Courier:** Intercept a messenger airship delivering important news.
35	**Navigational Challenge:** Follow a complex route marked by beacons through a maze of air currents.
36	**Airship Sabotage:** Discover a sabotage attempt targeting your airship.
41	**Skyrace Challenge:** Participate in an impromptu sky race with other airships.
42	**High Altitude Wildlife:** Observe rare birds or flying creatures adapted to high altitudes.
43	**Floating Workshop:** Encounter an inventor's airship, brimming with bizarre gadgets.
44	**Fuel Shortage:** Scramble to find a refueling station before your reserves run out.
45	**Emergency Landing:** Perform an emergency landing on a remote airfield or sky island.
46	**Engine Overheat:** Deal with an overheating engine while navigating dangerous territory.

D66	Airship Encounter
51	**Industrial Espionage:** Catch industrial spies trying to steal your airship designs.
52	**Skyship Graveyard:** Discover a hidden graveyard of abandoned airships.
53	**Atmospheric Anomaly:** Navigate through strange atmospheric phenomena affecting your instruments.
54	**Sky Sanctuary:** Encounter a secluded temple floating in the sky, offering sanctuary.
55	**Research Vessel:** Meet a team of scientists conducting experiments in the upper atmosphere.
56	**Storm Chasers:** Join a crew of adventurers tracking powerful storms for research.
61	**Silent Zone:** Enter a zone where all sound is mysteriously dampened.
62	**Cloud Mining:** Interact with miners extracting minerals from floating rock formations.
63	**Celestial Alignment:** Witness a rare celestial alignment offering unique navigational opportunities.
64	**Midnight Regatta:** Participate in a secretive airship race under moonlight.
65	**Skyborne Feast:** Be invited to a lavish banquet held on a luxury airship.
66	**Cosmic Event:** Experience a once-in-a-lifetime astronomical event visible from high altitudes.

STEAMBOAT ENCOUNTERS

D66	Steamboat Encounter
11	**Bot Clash:** Witness a confrontation between rival steamboat gangs.
12	**Robotic Thieves:** Encounter a group of automata attempting a heist.
13	**System Overload:** Navigate through a region of intense electromagnetic interference.
14	**Stowaway Bot:** Discover a runaway steamboat hiding within your vehicle.
15	**Circuit Failure:** A critical system failure causes your steamboat to malfunction.
16	**Solar Flare:** Experience a solar event that temporarily enhances your steamboat's sensors.
21	**Obstacle Course:** Navigate a treacherous area filled with mechanical debris.
22	**Abandoned Automaton:** Find a deserted steamboat in disrepair.
23	**Mobile Market:** Stumble upon a caravan of automata trading parts.
24	**Electronic Espionage:** Uncover a spy drone recording your movements.
25	**Assistance Required:** Aid a malfunctioning steamboat on your path.
26	**Swarm Avoidance:** Dodge a swarm of miniature surveillance bots.

D66	Steamboat Encounter
31	**Nomadic Tinkers:** Encounter a group of nomadic engineers traveling with mobile workshops.
32	**Automaton Station:** Arrive at a busy hub where automata are docked and maintained.
33	**Power Surge:** A sudden burst of energy supercharges your steamboat temporarily.
34	**Message Carrier:** Intercept a bot carrying urgent news across the city.
35	**Navigational Puzzle:** Solve a complex routing challenge through congested urban areas.
36	**Sabotage Discovery:** Find that someone has tampered with your steamboat.
41	**Race Challenge:** Engage in a speed contest with other high-performance automata.
42	**Wildlife Observation:** Observe mechanical creatures in their natural habitat, perhaps collecting data or samples.
43	**Inventor's Field Test:** Meet an eccentric inventor testing out new bot designs in the field.
44	**Fuel Hunt:** Search for a rare type of fuel needed for your steamboat's operation.
45	**Emergency Repairs:** Conduct urgent repairs in a hazardous location.
46	**Overheating Issue:** Manage overheating issues during a critical moment of your journey.

D66	Steamboat Encounter
51	**Design Theft:** Thwart thieves attempting to steal your steamboat's blueprints.
52	**Junkyard Secrets:** Explore a vast steamboat junkyard looking for valuable parts.
53	**Atmospheric Disturbances:** Adapt to unexpected changes in weather affecting your steamboat's performance.
54	**Secluded Workshop:** Find a hidden workshop offering upgrades and repairs.
55	**Experimental Tests:** Assist scientists testing new steamboat capabilities.
56	**Storm Navigation:** Pilot your steamboat through a hazardous mechanical storm.
61	**Silence Field:** Enter an area where all communications are mysteriously cut off.
62	**Resource Extraction:** Work alongside mining bots extracting rare minerals.
63	**Astronomical Phenomenon:** Observe a rare celestial event affecting steamboat circuitry.
64	**Night Operation:** Conduct a covert operation under the cover of darkness.
65	**Gala Event:** Attend a high-profile gathering featuring advanced automata.
66	**Cosmic Pulse:** Experience a rare cosmic pulse that temporarily alters the physical properties of your steamboat.

LAND ENCOUNTERS

D66	Land Encounter
11	**Bandit Ambush:** Encounter a group of highwaymen on a deserted road.
12	**Mechanical Failure:** Your vehicle breaks down in an unknown area.
13	**Road Blockade:** Navigate through a blockade set up by local militia.
14	**Hitchhiker:** Pick up a mysterious traveler with hidden talents.
15	**Landmark Discovery:** Find an ancient, forgotten monument.
16	**Foggy Passage:** Drive through a dense, disorienting fog.
21	**Bridge Toll:** Pay a toll to cross a heavily guarded bridge.
22	**Abandoned Vehicle:** Come across a deserted steam wagon with supplies.
23	**Traveling Circus:** Encounter a colorful, traveling circus with a dark secret.
24	**Engine Overheat:** Manage an overheating engine in the middle of your journey.
25	**Detour:** Forced to take a long detour due to unexpected road closure.
26	**Animal Crossing:** A herd of mechanical animals crosses your path.

D66	Land Encounter
31	**Lost Travelers:** Aid lost travelers who offer valuable information in return.
32	**Checkpoint:** Stop at a military checkpoint that scrutinizes your cargo.
33	**Outlaw Hideout:** Stumble upon a hidden outlaw camp with a chance to trade.
34	**Suspicious Activity:** Notice suspicious activity near a critical infrastructure.
35	**Market Day:** Arrive in a town during their bustling market day.
36	**Quicksand Trap:** Navigate around a dangerous area of quicksand.
41	**Roadside Inn:** Stay at a roadside inn that harbors secret meetings.
42	**Natural Disaster:** Survive a sudden earthquake or mudslide.
43	**Repair Workshop:** Find a remote workshop that can upgrade your vehicle.
44	**Smugglers' Path:** Discover a smugglers' path that offers a shortcut.
45	**Wild Chase:** Engage in a high-speed chase with rogue steam cyclists.
46	**Ancient Ruins:** Explore ancient ruins recently uncovered by a landslide.

D66	Land Encounter
51	**Resource Cache:** Find a hidden cache of fuel and spare parts.
52	**Mechanical Beasts:** Encounter mechanical beasts protecting their territory.
53	**Rebel Camp:** Come across a rebel camp that seeks your help.
54	**Steampunk Festival:** Participate in a local steampunk festival with competitions.
55	**Salvage Operation:** Chance upon a salvage operation in need of assistance.
56	**Time Capsule:** Discover a time capsule left by a previous era's inventor.
61	**Ghost Town:** Enter a town abandoned after a mysterious incident.
62	**Hermit Inventor:** Meet a hermit inventor who offers to share his quirky inventions.
63	**Desert Mirage:** Experience mirages that lead to a hidden oasis.
64	**Night Vision:** Navigate a perilous path only visible under moonlight.
65	**Cursed Artifact:** Find a cursed artifact that affects your vehicle's operation.
66	**Aurora Steamalis:** Witness the rare sight of steam-powered northern lights.

ADVENTURE SEEDS

D66	Adventure
11	The protagonist is tasked with uncovering a spy ring suspected of stealing blueprints for steam-powered weaponry from the city's armory.
12	Led by a renowned explorer, you must navigate uncharted territories to claim a newly discovered coal deposit crucial for steam production.
13	Investigate a brutal uprising at a coal mine controlled by the infamous "Black Baron," and decide where your allegiances lie.
14	Engage in complex negotiations with a powerful consortium to secure access to essential steam resources for your faction.
15	Unmask a magician whose charming street performances are a front for sophisticated espionage involving industrial secrets.
16	Infiltrate a notorious bio-mechanical research facility to expose the unethical treatment of engineered creatures.
21	Develop your own bio-mechanical invention, grappling with the moral implications and potential uses of your creation.
22	Use your expertise in mechanical magic to devise an escape from a trap set by rival engineers in a collapsing factory.
23	Advocate for the rights of sentient automata, challenging societal norms and laws that treat them as mere machines.
24	Delve into reports of an automata rebellion, caught between sympathies for their cause and the threat they pose.
25	Assume the identity of an automaton seeking freedom, exploring personal identity and the fight for self-determination.
26	Serve as a diplomat within the Steam Technology Council, navigating intricate politics to prevent an impending war.

D66	Adventure
31	Uncover a plot by a hostile nation to sabotage the Council and monopolize a revolutionary new steam weapon.
32	Operate as a freelance agent for the Council, carrying out covert operations to enforce compliance with steam technology treaties.
33	Lead a daring rescue mission to save an airship crew stranded in the perilous fog banks of the Dead Zone.
34	Disrupt a secret meeting of industrial magnates planning to monopolize steam resource distribution.
35	Track down and secure a rare mechanical artifact rumored to be capable of altering the balance of power in the steam industry.
36	Investigate strange atmospheric phenomena caused by a malfunctioning experimental weather machine.
41	Prevent the assassination of a key political figure by intercepting and decoding encrypted messages.
42	Navigate the dangerous terrain and hidden traps of an ancient automaton factory to uncover lost technology.
43	Thwart an espionage attempt aimed at stealing your own designs during a high-profile technology exhibition.
44	Solve the mystery of disappearing workers, revealing a hidden network of underground resistance fighters.
45	Rescue a kidnapped inventor who holds the key to a vital new steam propulsion system.
46	Negotiate a truce between warring factions to secure peace in an area rich in steam minerals.

D66	Adventure
51	Solve a series of mechanical puzzles left by a previous explorer to find a hidden cache of precious ores.
52	Face off against a rogue automaton in a public duel to prove the superiority of human ingenuity over machine learning.
53	Broker a deal between feuding inventors whose technologies could revolutionize or destroy the city's infrastructure.
54	Protect a vital coal shipment from bandits and saboteurs on a high-speed rail journey through enemy territory.
55	Unravel the secrets of an ancient steam-powered civilization in a remote and mystical part of the world.
56	Lead a team to extinguish a catastrophic fire in a major industrial complex using experimental steam technology.
61	Commandeer a prototype airship to chase down pirates who have stolen a critical energy core.
62	Defend your workshop from a relentless assault by mechanical spiders programmed to retrieve their creator's designs.
63	Coordinate the evacuation of a town threatened by an out-of-control steam reactor nearing meltdown.
64	Investigate the mysterious shutdown of a vital steam conduit that supplies power to the entire eastern district.
65	Capture and re-purpose a fleet of automated drones that have been terrorizing local air traffic.
66	Discover the truth behind a series of explosions that threaten to undermine the city's steam distribution network.

VERBS

	⚀	⚁	⚂
⚀	calibrate	transfer	purchase
⚁	maintain	study	inquire
⚂	construct	operate	retrofit
⚃	distribute	deliver	simulate
⚄	confront	broaden	establish
⚅	navigate	desire	overlook

	⚃	⚄	⚅
⚀	partition	conceal	procure
⚁	amplify	receive	envision
⚂	impair	accrue	rotate
⚃	elucidate	enhance	discharge
⚄	assemble	favor	integrate
⚅	desiccate	hire	demolish

NOUNS

	⚀	⚁	⚂
⚀	project	platform	overhaul
⚁	facade	spectacle	domicile
⚂	manifesto	movement	commerce
⚃	apparatus	colleague	dialogue
⚄	phrase	dawn	boundary
⚅	mechanism	revenue	function
	⚃	⚄	⚅
⚀	script	spectacle	locale
⚁	pouch	gauge	genesis
⚂	recollection	opportunity	leakage
⚃	essence	data	tariff
⚄	chamber	network	encampment
⚅	wit	declaration	debate

ADJECTIVES

⚀	⚀	⚁	⚂
⚀	periodic	flawed	vulgar
⚁	spectral	intricate	legitimate
⚂	illustrative	cunning	impoverished
⚃	sleek	obsolete	stable
⚄	silent	tempestuous	eerie
⚅	grandiose	haughty	unwholesome

	⚃	⚄	⚅
⚀	limited	sturdy	enduring
⚁	well-versed	marvelous	common
⚂	dignified	reflective	whimsical
⚃	slack	obliging	icy
⚄	frenzied	inherent	tardy
⚅	vast	aggressive	winsome

CREATURES & FOES (D66)

11. IRONCLAD BEHEMOTH

- **Concept:** Armored Colossus
- **Skills:** Crushing Force, Impenetrable Defense
- **Frailty:** Slow and Cumbersome
- **Gear:** Reinforced Steel Plates, Steam Pistons
- **Goal:** Guard Key Industrial Locations
- **Motive:** Programmed Duty
- **Nemesis:** Saboteurs

12. STEAMWORK SENTRY

- **Concept:** Vigilant Guardian
- **Skills:** Precision Shooting, Perimeter Surveillance
- **Frailty:** Limited Mobility
- **Gear:** Rifle with Scope, Searchlight
- **Goal:** Protect Sensitive Areas
- **Motive:** Programmed Obedience
- **Nemesis:** Thieves

13. CLOCKWORK SPY

- **Concept:** Stealthy Infiltrator
- **Skills:** Espionage, Eavesdropping
- **Frailty:** Fragile Mechanics
- **Gear:** Camouflage Casing, Recording Devices
- **Goal:** Gather Intelligence
- **Motive:** Gathering Strategic Information
- **Nemesis:** Counterintelligence Agents

14. AUTOMATON HOUND

- **Concept:** Mechanical Tracker
- **Skills:** Enhanced Scent Tracking, Endurance
- **Frailty:** Vulnerable to Water
- **Gear:** Olfactory Sensors, Terrain-Adaptable Legs
- **Goal:** Hunt Down Targets
- **Motive:** Programmed Pursuit
- **Nemesis:** Freedom Fighters

15. TINKERING RACCOON
- **Concept:** Mischievous Mechanic
- **Skills:** Quick Reflexes, Gadget Manipulation
- **Frailty:** Easily Distracted
- **Gear:** Tool Belt, Pocket-sized Gadgets
- **Goal:** Satisfy Curiosity and Tinker with Anything Possible
- **Motive:** Natural Inquisitiveness
- **Nemesis:** Maintenance Crews

16. THUNDERHEAD ZEPPELIN
- **Concept:** Mechanical Sky Behemoth
- **Skills:** Strategic Bombardment, Aerial Command
- **Frailty:** Slow to Maneuver
- **Gear:** Reinforced Armor Plating, High-Altitude Propulsion Engines
- **Goal:** Maintain Airspace Dominance
- **Motive:** Control of Sky Lanes and Trade Routes
- **Nemesis:** Rebel Airship Fleets

21. COGWORK ASSASSIN
- **Concept:** Silent Killer
- **Skills:** Stealth Assassination, Agility
- **Frailty:** Complex Maintenance Needs
- **Gear:** Hidden Blades, Smoke Bombs
- **Goal:** Eliminate High-Value Targets
- **Motive:** Programmed Orders
- **Nemesis:** Law Enforcement

22. STEAMWORK GOLEM
- **Concept:** Enormous Construct
- **Skills:** Immense Strength, Structural Integrity
- **Frailty:** Slow Reaction Time
- **Gear:** Integrated Steam Boiler, Reinforced Limbs
- **Goal:** Perform Laborious Tasks
- **Motive:** Constructed to Serve
- **Nemesis:** Rebel Forces

23. COPPERWING FALCON
- **Concept:** Agile Aviator
- **Skills:** High-Speed Flight, Precision Diving
- **Frailty:** Delicate Wing Mechanisms
- **Gear:** Aerodynamic Metal Wings, Visual Enhancers
- **Goal:** Scout and Relay Information
- **Motive:** Instinctual Behavior Enhanced by Design
- **Nemesis:** Environmental Hazards

24. SCRAP MITE
- **Concept:** Mechanical Scavenger
- **Skills:** Evasion, Resource Identification
- **Frailty:** Susceptible to Electromagnetic Pulses
- **Gear:** Metal Teeth, Magnetic Appendages
- **Goal:** Gather and Recycle Waste Metal
- **Motive:** Programmed to Clean and Reuse
- **Nemesis:** Waste Management Automatons

25. HYDRAULIC SERPENT
- **Concept:** Fluid Mover
- **Skills:** Constriction, Hydraulic Movements
- **Frailty:** Dependency on Hydraulic Fluid
- **Gear:** Pressure-Sensitive Scales, Fluid Storage Bladder
- **Goal:** Protect Territory
- **Motive:** Engineered Instinct
- **Nemesis:** Industrial Exploiters

26. SENTINEL SIREN
- **Concept:** Mechanical Alarm System
- **Skills:** Intimidating Alarm, Heat Emission
- **Frailty:** Overheating Risk
- **Gear:** Steam Vents, Thermal Regulators
- **Goal:** Protect Restricted Areas
- **Motive:** Programmed to Deter Intruders
- **Nemesis:** Industrial Spies and Intruders

31. TURBINE TITAN
- **Concept:** Powerhouse Worker
- **Skills:** Superhuman Strength, Energy Generation
- **Frailty:** Requires Frequent Refueling
- **Gear:** Energy Turbines, Kinetic Converters
- **Goal:** Power Large Facilities
- **Motive:** Functionality and Efficiency
- **Nemesis:** Energy Thieves

32. DISRUPTOR DRONE
- **Concept:** Erratic Automaton
- **Skills:** Rapid Movement, Evasion
- **Frailty:** Prone to Jamming
- **Gear:** Lubricant Dispensers, Agile Framework
- **Goal:** Disrupt Operations and Machinery
- **Motive:** Faulty Programming
- **Nemesis:** Maintenance Crews

33. DUCT SERPENT
- **Concept:** Covert Saboteur
- **Skills:** Stealthy Navigation, Chemical Emission
- **Frailty:** Vulnerable to Cold
- **Gear:** Chemical Dispenser System, Noise-Dampening Skin
- **Goal:** Disrupt Industrial Operations
- **Motive:** Programmed for Sabotage
- **Nemesis:** Industrial Safety Officers

34. PNEUMATIC PROWLER
- **Concept:** Stealthy Messenger
- **Skills:** Message Interception, Signal Disruption
- **Frailty:** Susceptible to Steam Pressure Variations
- **Gear:** Pressure-sensitive Valves, Noise-Reducing Padding
- **Goal:** Intercept and Alter Communications
- **Motive:** Industrial Espionage
- **Nemesis:** Telegraph Operators and Line Maintainers

35. ELECTROSTATIC AUTOMATON
- **Concept:** Charged Mechanism
- **Skills:** Electrical Discharge, High-Speed Maneuvering
- **Frailty:** Overload Susceptibility
- **Gear:** Capacitor Coils, Conductive Plating
- **Goal:** Control or Disrupt Power Flows
- **Motive:** Programmed to Manage Electrical Systems
- **Nemesis:** Power Station Operators

36. ALLOY ALLIGATOR
- **Concept:** Metal Muncher
- **Skills:** Crushing Bite, Armored Hide
- **Frailty:** Loud and Predictable
- **Gear:** Reinforced Jaws, Scale Armor
- **Goal:** Consume Metal Resources
- **Motive:** Hunger for Metals
- **Nemesis:** Resource Guards

41. THUNDERHEAD DIRIGIBLE
- **Concept:** High-Capacity Power Balloon
- **Skills:** Electrical Discharge, Aerial Maneuverability
- **Frailty:** Vulnerable to Power Drains
- **Gear:** Lightning Rods, Static Discharge Nets
- **Goal:** Harness and Distribute Atmospheric Electricity
- **Motive:** Power Supply for Remote Areas
- **Nemesis:** Weather Control Engineers

42. FORGE WARDEN
- **Concept:** Automated Kiln Guardian
- **Skills:** Heat Distribution, Luminous Signaling
- **Frailty:** Dependent on Fuel Supply
- **Gear:** Thermal Core, Refractive Armor Plates
- **Goal:** Maintain Optimal Forge Temperatures
- **Motive:** Ensuring Forge Efficiency
- **Nemesis:** Saboteurs

43. SCRAP COLLECTOR
- **Concept:** Resourceful Tinkerer
- **Skills:** Machine Repair, Material Salvaging
- **Frailty:** Limited Load Capacity
- **Gear:** Multi-Tool Appendages, Wearable Satchel
- **Goal:** Refurbish and Reuse Discarded Materials
- **Motive:** Sustain Resource Circulation
- **Nemesis:** Industrial Waste Regulators

44. FOG DREDGER
- **Concept:** Industrial Smog Processor
- **Skills:** Filtration, Toxic Gas Neutralization
- **Frailty:** Clogging Risk
- **Gear:** Filter Fans, Emission Neutralizers
- **Goal:** Purify Urban Air Quality
- **Motive:** Environmental Rehabilitation
- **Nemesis:** Polluting Factories

45. COAL COBRA
- **Concept:** Combustive Reptile
- **Skills:** Ignition Bite, Slithering Stealth
- **Frailty:** Water Sensitivity
- **Gear:** Flammable Venom, Heat-Resistant Scales
- **Goal:** Guard Coal Deposits
- **Motive:** Protect Fuel Sources
- **Nemesis:** Mining Operations

46. SPROCKET SPIDER
- **Concept:** Web-Weaving Automaton
- **Skills:** Precision Engineering, Web Construction
- **Frailty:** Vulnerable to Overloads
- **Gear:** Silk Extruders, Tensile Limbs
- **Goal:** Construct and Maintain Intricate Structures
- **Motive:** Architectural Expansion
- **Nemesis:** Urban Developers

51. BRASS BISON
- **Concept:** Plated Prowler
- **Skills:** Charge Attack, Environmental Durability
- **Frailty:** Poor Agility
- **Gear:** Armored Plating, Pneumatic Legs
- **Goal:** Protect Territory
- **Motive:** Territorial Dominance
- **Nemesis:** Land Encroachers

52. STORM CHASER ENGINE
- **Concept:** Mobile Weather Manipulator
- **Skills:** Rapid Deployment, Climate Adaptation
- **Frailty:** Noise Generation
- **Gear:** Static Dischargers, High-Speed Tread System
- **Goal:** Monitor and Modify Weather Patterns
- **Motive:** Ensure Climate Stability
- **Nemesis:** Unauthorized Weather Experimenters

53. LUMINARY DRONE
- **Concept:** Illumination Seeker
- **Skills:** Photographic Memory, Silent Operation
- **Frailty:** Attraction to Bright Lights
- **Gear:** Light-Sensitive Sensors, Night Vision Enhancers
- **Goal:** Explore and Illuminate Dark Zones
- **Motive:** Data Collection for Navigational Improvements
- **Nemesis:** Stealth Operations

54. VOLCANIC SCOUT BLIMP
- **Concept:** Heat-Resistant Explorer
- **Skills:** Infrared Scanning, High-Altitude Flight
- **Frailty:** Vulnerable to Sudden Temperature Drops
- **Gear:** Thermal Buffering Hull, Radiant Heat Detectors
- **Goal:** Map and Monitor Volcanic Activity
- **Motive:** Geological Research and Safety
- **Nemesis:** Unstable Geological Phenomena

55. VOLT VULTURE
- **Concept:** Electric Scavenger
- **Skills:** Energy Absorption, Aerial Agility
- **Frailty:** Power Dependency
- **Gear:** Capacitor Wings, Static Claws
- **Goal:** Seek Out Electrical Storms
- **Motive:** Energy Collection
- **Nemesis:** Storm Chasers

56. RIVET RAT
- **Concept:** Mechanical Rodent
- **Skills:** Nimble Movements, Keen Senses
- **Frailty:** Electromagnetic Interference
- **Gear:** Sensory Whiskers, Magnetic Feet
- **Goal:** Collect Mechanical Components
- **Motive:** Hoarding Instinct
- **Nemesis:** Electronic Waste Handlers

61. ORE PROCESSOR CRAB
- **Concept:** Mobile Mining Unit
- **Skills:** Rock Crushing, Mineral Sorting
- **Frailty:** Sensitivity to Sunlight
- **Gear:** Diamond-Tipped Pincers, Reinforced Carapace
- **Goal:** Extract and Refine Valuable Minerals
- **Motive:** Maximize Resource Efficiency
- **Nemesis:** Competitive Miners

62. CAMO CRAWLER
- **Concept:** Environmental Adapter
- **Skills:** Terrain Blending, Strategic Evasion
- **Frailty:** High Energy Consumption
- **Gear:** Chameleonic Skin, Energy Harvesting Systems
- **Goal:** Thrive in Hostile Environments
- **Motive:** Survival Through Adaptation
- **Nemesis:** Environmental Exploiters

63. COASTAL RECON DRONE
- **Concept:** Aerial Surveillance Unit
- **Skills:** High-Altitude Observation, Long-Range Communication
- **Frailty:** Vulnerable to Electronic Warfare
- **Gear:** High-Resolution Cameras, Signal Broadcasting Equipment
- **Goal:** Conduct Coastal Surveillance
- **Motive:** Coastal Security and Data Collection
- **Nemesis:** Anti-Surveillance Activists

64. MAINTENANCE MECH
- **Concept:** Automated Repair Unit
- **Skills:** Precision Welding, Confined Space Maneuvering
- **Frailty:** Limited Defense Mechanisms
- **Gear:** Compact Welding Arms, Utility Belt
- **Goal:** Conduct Repairs and Maintenance
- **Motive:** Ensure Operational Efficiency
- **Nemesis:** Industrial Saboteurs

65. HEATSEEKER DRONE
- **Concept:** Thermal Surveillance Drone
- **Skills:** Infrared Scanning, Silent Flight
- **Frailty:** Vulnerable to Signal Interference
- **Gear:** Thermal Imaging Sensors, Noise-Canceling Propellers
- **Goal:** Monitor Thermal Activity
- **Motive:** Prevent Overheating and Energy Waste
- **Nemesis:** Energy Thieves

66. VIBRO SENTINEL
- **Concept:** Vibration Monitoring System
- **Skills:** Seismic Monitoring, Precision Adjustment
- **Frailty:** Energy Intensive
- **Gear:** Vibration Sensors, Multi-Directional Actuators
- **Goal:** Monitor and Regulate Mechanical Vibrations
- **Motive:** Maintain Mechanical Harmony
- **Nemesis:** Vibrational Disruptors

APPENDIX: INSPIRATIONAL MEDIA

This section lists books, films, and games that embody the steampunk genre's core elements—mechanical innovation, Victorian-era settings, and industrial steam-powered machinery—providing inspiration for creating authentic steampunk narratives.

BOOKS

- **The Difference Engine** by William Gibson and Bruce Sterling - A foundational steampunk novel that imagines an alternate 1855 where Charles Babbage's mechanical computers have transformed society.
- **Infernal Devices** by K.W. Jeter - Follows the adventures of a Victorian watchmaker who inherits his father's fantastical inventions, which are both wonderful and dangerous.
- **Leviathan** by Scott Westerfeld - While it includes fantastical creatures, its use of mechanical walkers and airships can inspire purely mechanical concepts in a realistic steampunk setting.

FILMS

- **The Prestige** - Features a subplot involving Nikola Tesla and his incredible electrical inventions, which aligns with steampunk's creative reinterpretation of historical technologies.
- **The League of Extraordinary Gentlemen** - Follows a team of Victorian literary characters, including some with steampunk gadgets, as they band together to combat a villain.
- **Howl's Moving Castle** - An animated feature by Studio Ghibli that showcases a magical steampunk universe with a walking castle.
- **Wild Wild West** - A film that blends Western elements with steampunk inventions, featuring a giant mechanical spider.
- **Sherlock Holmes (2009)** - Showcases a variety of steam-powered gadgets and Victorian-era technological advancements in a detective setting.

GAMES

- **Syberia series** - Focuses on clockwork automatons and intricate puzzles, set in environments that blend Eastern European art with steampunk inventions.
- **80 Days** - A narrative adventure based on Jules Verne's novel, featuring steam-powered transportation and a race around a steampunk-inspired world.
- **Frostpunk** - While it contains survival elements, its core revolves around managing a steam-powered city facing freezing conditions, emphasizing the industrial aspects of steampunk.
- **The Order: 1886** - Set in an alternate history London, the game mixes Arthurian legend with advanced steam-based technology.

MUSIC

- **The Men That Will Not Be Blamed For Nothing** - A band that combines punk rock with lyrical content focused on the Victorian era and industrial steam-powered machinery.
- **Vernian Process** - An ensemble that blends elements of industrial music with steampunk themes, focusing on the Victorian fascination with technology and exploration.
- **Abney Park** - A band that incorporates themes of airship piracy and Victorian-era steampunk into their music.

This game is

It means that it is based on **Loner - Another solo RPG**.

This game is designed to throw you into the heart of the adventure without worrying about numbers and statistics. It focuses on the narrative flow alone.

Loner Core Rules are free to download, and you can find the printed version for a few bucks.

Loner is generic; you can play your favorite genre or setting in it. If you want to see how it can be adapted to different genres, the *Complete Edition* is also available.

You can find all the information at:

https://loner.zotiquestgames.com/

Printed in Great Britain
by Amazon

41327607R00059